BEST LAID PLANS

LAUREN BLAKELY

Copyright © 2019 by Lauren Blakely
LaurenBlakely.com
Cover Design by © Helen Williams, photo by Rafa Catala
First Edition Book

All rights reserved. Without limiting the rights under copyright reserved above, no part of this publication may be reproduced, stored in or introduced into a retrieval system, or transmitted, in any form, or by any means (electronic, mechanical, photocopying, recording, or otherwise) without the prior written permission of both the copyright owner and the above publisher of this book.

This is a work of fiction. Names, characters, places, brands, media, and incidents are either the product of the author's imagination or are used fictitiously. The author acknowledges the trademarked status and trademark owners of various products referenced in this work of fiction, which have been used without permission. The publication/use of these trademarks is not authorized, associated with, or sponsored by the trademark owners. This ebook is licensed for your personal use only. This ebook may not be re-sold or given away to other people. If you would like to share this book with another person, please purchase an additional copy for each person you share it with. If you are reading this book and did not purchase it, or it was not purchased for your use only, then you should return it and purchase your own copy. Thank you for respecting the author's work.

ALSO BY LAUREN BLAKELY

Big Rock Series

Big Rock

Mister O

Well Hung

Full Package

Joy Ride

Hard Wood

One Love Series dual-POV Standalones

The Sexy One

The Only One

The Hot One

Sports Romance

Most Valuable Playboy

Most Likely to Score

Standalones

The Knocked Up Plan

Stud Finder

The V Card

Wanderlust

Come As You Are

Part-Time Lover

The Real Deal

Unbreak My Heart

The Break Up Album

21 Stolen Kisses

Out of Bounds

Unzipped

Birthday Suit

Best Laid Plans

The Feel Good Factor

The Dating Proposal

Satisfaction Guaranteed

Never Have I Ever

Instant Gratification

The Heartbreakers Series
Once Upon a Real Good Time

Once Upon a Sure Thing

Once Upon a Wild Fling

The Caught Up in Love Series
Caught Up In Us

Pretending He's Mine
Playing With Her Heart

Stars In Their Eyes Duet
My Charming Rival
My Sexy Rival

The No Regrets Series
The Thrill of It
The Start of Us
Every Second With You

The Seductive Nights Series
First Night (Julia and Clay, prequel novella)
Night After Night (Julia and Clay, book one)
After This Night (Julia and Clay, book two)
One More Night (Julia and Clay, book three)
A Wildly Seductive Night (Julia and Clay novella, book 3.5)

The Joy Delivered Duet
Nights With Him (A standalone novel about Michelle and Jack)
Forbidden Nights (A standalone novel about Nate and Casey)

The Sinful Nights Series
Sweet Sinful Nights

Sinful Desire

Sinful Longing

Sinful Love

The Fighting Fire Series

Burn For Me (Smith and Jamie)

Melt for Him (Megan and Becker)

Consumed By You (Travis and Cara)

The Jewel Series

A two-book sexy contemporary romance series

The Sapphire Affair

The Sapphire Heist

PROLOGUE
ARDEN

I'm most definitely a planner, but I never planned to be a good girl.

Honestly, I didn't even think twice about good girls versus naughty ones. I always figured with sex and love, you could have it all.

That's what we're taught as women, right?

You can be prim and proper during the day and wild and daring at night. Or the other way around. Whatever floats your banana boat.

But somehow over the years, I inadvertently landed on the "nice" half of the divide, so squarely in the good-girl camp I'm practically the poster child of *oh-so-sweet*, and I can't seem to get a crack at the other side.

Only, I keep peeking over the fence, peering, wondering.

What if the grass is greener? What if I'm missing

out on something better in the bedroom and, by extension, something better in life and love?

There's only one way to find out.

Ask.

The trouble is, when it -comes time to woman up and make a request for what I want to try at the ice cream stand of sexual flavors and favors, I wind up with so much more than I bargained for.

More than I'm ready for . . .

And with so much more to lose than I ever expected.

Guess I'm about to learn if it's better to be naughty or to be nice.

1

ARDEN

A year ago

You can never go wrong with cheese.

Or crackers, for that matter.

Add in grapes, hummus, olives, Marcona almonds, and strawberries, and you're good to go.

Plus, wine. Because . . . *wine*.

As I tug the corners of a red-and-white checkered blanket neatly across the grass, I'm 100 percent pleased with the spread.

Wicker picnic basket with adorable handles? Check.

Tasty food and treats? Check.

And the woman he wants? Double check.

Plus, I'm wearing his favorite outfit.

Well, David probably prefers me in heels and lingerie, on account of being male and all. But I'm surrounded by bushes, bugs, and trees, and you can't wear heels on a hiking trail.

If I did, I'd be a complete nitwit.

Generally, I try to avoid nitwittery, partial or complete.

And I try to embrace looking pretty for my man. That's why I'm sporting a dress, since he likes dresses and the easy access they afford. This summery blue number with white polka dots has a cute breast-hugging bodice and a skirt that's the right length. Navy-blue Converse sneakers complete the casual but cute look.

Picnic couture, I like to call it.

A platoon of butterflies flaps around in my chest, but I don't let them wind me up or worry me. Taking a deep, calming breath, I remind myself that I have fantastic plans to take our relationship to the next level, and I have a good feeling David wants the same. He's given me every indication we're on the same page.

Well, every indication, bar asking me himself, but the number of times he's remarked on how helpful it would be to have a toothbrush, deodorant, and the farm-fresh eggs he likes for breakfast at my place are indication enough.

How could he not want to move in together?

We're simpatico, like mornings and coffee, movies and popcorn.

Moving in together is the next step on the path to "I do." Today, I plan to let him know that's what I envision for us—sharing a place, sharing a life, and eventually sharing a name.

One step at a time, but the first one starts with something along the lines of:

Would you like to move in with me because I picked up those coffee filters you like so much and I'd be happy to make you a cup of joe every morning?

I already have the filters on the kitchen counter, ready for his coffee-loving heart.

Checking my phone for the time, I bounce on my toes in excitement. He'll be here any minute.

I whistle a short tune.

Fine, he'll be here in one more minute.

I peek inside the basket once more. A perfect spread for a Sunday lunch here along Silver Phoenix Lake, the water reflecting the bright sun and the birds chirping in the trees.

Another minute ticks by, and I smooth my hand along my skirt and double-check the wineglasses. The crisp sauvignon blanc I picked out is delish for today's festivities. I happen to be fantastic at wine pairings, and I know this one is ideal.

I stand, crunch across the twigs and grass to the trail, and peer down the path.

No sign of David.

No matter. He'll be here soon. I return to the blanket. I shield my eyes as I look to the sky, reminding myself to enjoy the view, to savor the great outdoors.

I do that for fifteen stinking minutes.

I try not to get wound up. It's entirely possible he received a call from the hospital. That happens, and I'm used to it. I'm a good ER resident's girlfriend.

I check my phone. Odd. There's no message from him. But if there'd been an emergency, he probably wouldn't have had time to call me. And really, don't we all want a society where doctors are focused on saving lives rather than alerting their women of their whereabouts?

But he *is* off today, and there's also *this* cheese.

I don't want it out *all day*, especially since I already sliced it.

I should send him a text. What if he has the location wrong? I check the message I sent him yesterday, where I asked him to meet me in this little nook of the woods, a few feet off the trail, then tap out a quick text.

Hey, handsome. Can't wait to see you! Just wanted to make sure —

I stop typing when I hear footsteps, and my heart runs in circles.

"Hey, Arden."

I smile giddily. He's here at last, walking past the tree, and when my eyes land on his handsome face, his dark hair, his eyes that I know so well, I chide myself for worrying.

Of course he's here. The fact that he's been a little busy, a little distant lately means nothing. I pop up and practically run to him, throwing my arms around his neck.

He's stiff at first then hugs me back. "Sorry I'm late. I was at the gym."

What?

He was at the ever-loving gym?

"I hope you had the best workout ever, then," I say, keeping my tone chipper, even though inside I'm thinking that's rude with a capital R. But I have things to do and plans for us, so I move on. "And I'm glad you made it. I have a picnic lunch with all your favorites." I jut out my hip then whisper, "Including me. It's private here too. We can eat and chat and maybe more . . ." A flush spreads across my cheeks as my voice trails off in invitation. The suggestion feels a little risqué to me, but I'd like to try a little risqué-ness. I've never had sex outdoors, and I honestly wouldn't mind trying something new. I shiver at the thought.

David looks away, scratching his jaw. "Yeah, that's the thing, Arden."

"What's the thing?" My pitch rises as worry shoots up in me. His tone is saying something before his words do, and that something isn't what I want to hear.

He sighs, smiles sympathetically, and then fingers a strand of my blonde hair. "You're so sweet. Seriously. You're like the nicest girl I've ever met."

There's a but coming. A big fat but.

I swallow past the stone in my throat. "Nice is good, right?" I sound as if I'm white-knuckling a steering wheel so I don't drive a car off the side of the road.

David leans closer, lets go of my hair, and drops his voice like he's prepping to say something grave to a patient. "But I like naughty better, so I don't think this is going to work out."

The earth slips beneath me. The sky falls. My plans crater. This was not on my schedule for today.

Especially since he has no idea how much I'd be interested in trying something new in bed. But he's never asked.

"You never said you liked naughty better," I point out as my stomach twists and hurt claws its way up my throat.

He shakes his head, making sure I don't miss his meaning as he points from him to me. "I shouldn't have to say it. Naughty should come naturally."

"What? You shouldn't have to say it? How else would I know what you wanted?"

He laughs gently. "Even if I said it, it doesn't matter. You're too good. It's your natural state. You don't have a naughty bone in your body."

"Oh, I do. I definitely have several." He's wrong. He's so wrong. All my naughty bones are just waiting to be used.

"You're so adorable. That's why I don't think you and I will work out."

Of course we can work. All we have to do is talk. Maybe he's been working too hard in the ER. Maybe he's stress-tired. Surely that must be it.

I place a hand on his chest. "We can talk about this. Work this out. Try all sorts of new things in the bedroom, or even *here*. This is the first time you've mentioned it, but I'm up for it. I was literally thinking about other uses for this blanket before you showed up. I know we haven't had sex outdoors, but we should try new things in the bedroom and out of the bedroom." I take a deep breath and go for it. "After all, I love you and I want you to move in with me. Isn't that where we are headed?"

Not exactly how I planned to ask him, but clearly I have to launch the parachute quickly and try to save our plane from tumbling out of the sky.

He smiles even more sympathetically, quite possibly full of abject pity for me. This isn't going to end how I want it to at all. I am the biggest fool in the land.

"Look at you. So good to me up until the end. That's why it took me so long to say this. Because you treat me like a king, and you're so damn sweet. It almost makes me want to stay." He sighs. "But you're too vanilla." He pats my head like I'm a pet, and evidently I'm the Maltese he's not taking home from the pound instead of the chocolate lab he really wants.

I jerk my head away from him. "Don't pat me like a dog."

"I was just trying to be nice."

"Oh, don't even use that word with me right now. '*Nice*,'" I hiss, even as tears threaten my throat, clogging my voice.

He ignores me, gesturing to the picnic spread. "Food looks good. Can I grab some cheese and crackers before I go? I do love Gouda."

Shock slams into me, radiating to every pore. I can't even speak or scream—*no, you can't have the Gouda, you jackass*—because I'm so floored by his callous request.

The hungry jerk takes my silence as a yes and helps himself, bending to grab a few slices of cheese from the basket and a couple of crackers. My eyes burn with tears, and I want to smack his impromptu snack out of his hand, but I can't because my blood has turned sluggish.

David turns to go, and I'm in quicksand, unable to move or speak. As his footsteps fade, something new replaces the shock.

Anger.

He took my cheese.

He took my freaking Gouda cheese.

"You don't deserve cheese. You don't deserve chocolate. You don't deserve vanilla," I shout between sobs, then grab the bottle of wine, open it, and guzzle a needy gulp.

A crunch of leaves sounds from the trail, and my heart speeds into overdrive.

He's returned. He realized his mistake. He's

going to ask me to stay with him. I fasten on a smile, swipe my cheeks, and prepare to let him grovel.

First, he'll apologize for taking my Gouda.

Second, he'll take back that stupid vanilla comment.

Third, he'll say he's sorry he never piped up before about all these naughty bones that need tending to.

Then, and only then, will I let him enjoy the picnic of me.

I peer down the path, searching for my man.

But he's still gone, and I'm still alone, dumped at a picnic lunch, when I planned to ask him to move in with me. My only company is a bird, an industrious robin, scouring the trail.

Why should he suffer because I've been ditched? I toss him a cracker and he pecks at it.

"Have a snack," I mutter.

Another robin swoops down, joining his buddy on the dirt to enjoy the unexpected snack I'd planned to share with David.

The bastard.

How does he know I'm too sweet? He never asked me to be naughty. I wouldn't mind trying. But he didn't say a word about what he wanted. Am I supposed to be a mind reader? I don't think so.

"You could have asked," I mumble.

But I'm not in the mood to mumble. I'm in the mood to shout and stomp and throw. I don't give a damn if this is childish. It's cathartic, and right now I need to let go. I spin around, grab more cheese slices, and fling them in David's direction, even though he's probably miles away now.

"Take that." I catapult one through the air.

"Here's another." I launch a cracker, then a slice of cheese.

More. I need more. This feels good. This feels so damn good. I bend to grab another hunk of cheese, then spin around and slingshot my arm to send it down the trail. Like a gunslinger, I fire, sending the dairy flying.

Only it doesn't land on the trail.

The Gouda lands square in the middle of a chest.

A man's chest.

Oops.

I cringe, lifting my gaze. I'm greeted by the sight of the man known as the Lucky Falls Panty-Melter. Star of the fireman calendar. Resident charmer. All-around ladies' man. Dark-blond hair, soulful blue eyes, and a body that could advertise all the workouts in the world.

Kill me now.

Of all the people to run into. Of all the guys in this godforsaken town to inadvertently thwack with a piece of cheese. The bare-chested Gabe Harrison wears running shorts, sneakers, and a fine sheen of sweat glistening on his pecs.

As well as a slice of Gouda that sticks momentarily to his chest.

Stopping short, he surveys me and what's left of

the cheese and crackers, then his sternum, plucking the food from his skin like this happens every day and it's no big deal. "If you're going to turn more of the cheese and crackers into projectile missiles, allow me to help."

"I'm so, so sorry," I choke out, and the dam breaks.

The waterworks have been let loose, and anger has turned to sadness.

Tears fall as I sink down onto the blanket, crying into my cheese and crackers. Who cares if he's the town playboy? It's not like I'm on anyone's naughty or nice list right now anyway. It's not as if I'm looking for anything but a shoulder to cry on.

He drops down and wraps a strong arm around me. "Hey there. You want to talk about it?"

I can't talk because I'm too busy crying the Nile onto his broad, slicked chest, the site of the cheese bullet I lobbed at him.

2
GABE

Some women are silent criers. Some are snifflers, gently dabbing away at barely-there tears. And some are epic bawlers. Snot, soaked tissues, streams of water sluicing down their cheeks—the whole nine yards.

Then there's Arden East. She's going to need a new category. Because holy shit. I've encountered more than my fair share of tears in my line of work, but never enough to refill a reservoir.

She cries and cries and cries, and when she's maybe, possibly, almost finished replenishing the Pacific Ocean, she launches another pair of geysers from her eyes.

Judging from the picnic blanket and the food, I have a wild hunch her man disappointed her.

Badly.

In my field, I've learned plenty about how to handle this kind of sadness.

You need to let the tears fall, plain and simple.

After a few more minutes, she starts to quiet. "I'm so stupid," she blurts, the first sign that she's nearing the end of the crying jag.

"Of course you're not stupid. Why would you say that?"

"I thought . . . he wanted . . . to be . . . with me."

David.

She's been dating one of the ER docs. He's a solid doc, but that's about all I know of David Green. Except now he's most likely a dickhead, since he's the one who disappointed her badly. Who makes a woman cry like this but a guy who deserves the Dickhead of the Year Award?

"I made a picnic for him, and he dumped me." She swipes her palms against her cheeks. "He showed up and broke up with me, and he still asked for a piece of cheese."

My brow knits. "Seriously?"

"He said I was too nice. He didn't want to be with me, but he still wanted a cracker. Apparently, my food is enough for him, but I'm not."

I scoff. "I'm pretty sure that goes against all the codes and bylaws in the handbook of *How to Treat A Woman.*"

Arden's chocolate-brown eyes are shot with red, but they twinkle the slightest bit. "I'm pretty sure I'd like to chuck that handbook at the back of his head. Please tell me it comes in hardcover?"

I smile, pleased she's retained her sense of humor

in the face of the ultimate bonehead move. "It does, and also, on behalf of all men everywhere, I want to let you know that he's officially won the Dickhead of the Year Award. The guy committee has unanimously voted for him to receive it because the kind of shit he pulled gives men a bad name."

She offers a contrite smile. "That's why I was throwing the cheese. I'm sorry I hit you."

"I'm just glad it wasn't the bottle of wine you were practicing your shot put skills with. Wait. I don't want to give you any ideas." I grab the open wine bottle and hide it behind me.

"I promise I won't throw the wine at you." She cracks a grin through the tears.

Carefully, I set the wine back on the blanket. "Or almonds. Those can pack a punch too. You might have taken an eye out."

"I do have good aim." She laughs, then it morphs into a mournful sigh as she swats at the remnants of a final tear. "And I was going to ask him to move in with me."

I drop the attempt at humor, squeezing her shoulder. Even if the guy's a first-class jackass, she truly liked him, and that's nothing to joke about. "I'm sorry, Arden. You must be hurting a ton right now."

An errant sniffle sounds from her, and she nods. "I am. I wanted it all to go so perfectly."

My heart aches for her, for the effort she made, for the hope she must have had when she planned today. "It does look perfect." I take a cursory glance at the meal.

"He didn't think it was perfect enough."

I peer behind me, impressed with the spread she packed, from the wicker basket, to the wine and the glasses, all the way to the cloth napkins. Damn, this woman is a thorough planner and some kind of sweetheart in the girlfriend department. Inside the basket, I spot a container of hummus and three kinds of olives, along with the almonds and more cheese and crackers.

My stomach rumbles. "Any man who doesn't realize the value of you, almonds, and olives doesn't deserve to have lunch, breakfast, or dinner with you. Ever."

"Thank you." Her whispered voice is soft and pretty.

Hell, even with her splotchy, tear-stained cheeks, she's still so damn pretty.

Fact is, I thought she was lovely to look at the night I met her a year ago, shortly after I moved to town. Pretty and witty and sharp, but very taken, so I didn't think twice about her.

Today, she's still pretty, and now she's single.

Wait.

Chill the hell out, Brain. It's not cool to think a woman is pretty when she's crying her eyes out over another man.

I wipe those dickhead thoughts from my head. I don't want to give David competition for the dickhead prize.

"You really think he doesn't deserve me?" Her tone is wobbly.

"I know he doesn't." I point at the food. "Every decent man knows when a woman makes you a picnic, you damn well better eat it, and you will most certainly enjoy it."

A small smile seems to sneak across her face. "It was a nice picnic." She unleashes a sob again, tripping over that adjective. "*Nice*. He said I was too nice. Who's too nice? How is it possible to be too nice?"

I set a hand on her lower back, gently rubbing. "Nice is what we should all aspire to be."

She breathes heavily, clenches her jaw, and nods fiercely as if she's deciding she's done with tears. "Exactly, and my picnic is awesome, and he doesn't deserve it."

"No way. He doesn't even deserve a cracker that fell on the ground or the cheese from my chest."

Her lips quirk up, and she laughs in spite of herself, it seems. "Don't tempt me, Gabe. Now I want to serve him sweaty cheese and dirty crackers if he ever shows up for a wine and cheese night at the store," she says, and I picture the bookshop she owns in the center of town.

"It'll be our little secret that you have such a naughty side." Her eyes seem to sparkle appreciatively when I say that word—*naughty*.

I gesture to the meal. "This delicious spread should not go to waste," I say, hinting not at all subtly, since I'd like a bite of some of these goodies. "Don't know if you're aware, but I have had a bottomless appetite since I was born. I can pretty much always eat."

"And I like to reward hearty appetites." She grabs a slice of cheese and a cracker then hands them to me. "This picnic is definitely not for any recipients of the Dickhead of the Year Award." She gives a tough little lift of her chin.

"That's the spirit."

I smile widely at her, then pop the treat into my mouth. After I chew, I declare it the best cracker in the land.

It's a cracker, for fuck's sake.

But Arden is smiling again.

And that's the least I can do.

I don't know David from Adam. I don't know their relationship whatsoever. But I know this: the woman made him a meal, put on a pretty dress, and placed her heart on this red-and-white checkered blanket.

However he ended things, leaving her like this was a jackass move of the highest order. If he didn't have the sensitivity to know that, the least I can do is show her that some men do have the common courtesy to enjoy a feast prepared by a good woman.

Grabbing a napkin, I dab at the remnants of tears on her cheeks, and she whispers her thanks.

We dine, and we chat, and I steer the conversation to innocuous topics. "Favorite cheese? If you had to pick one cheese for the rest of your life, what would it be?"

She shoots me a you-can't-be-serious look after that question. "Are you trying to be cruel and unusual?"

I laugh, waving it off. "You're right. Having only one kind of cheese forever and ever does sound like a fresh new hell."

She nudges me with her elbow. "Exactly." She rolls her eyes. "Next thing you know, you'll be trying to get me to choose only one wine for the rest of my days."

I hold up my hands in surrender. "I've learned my lesson. I swear."

"Good." She lowers her voice. "For the record, it'd be a white."

"Ah, so you do have a favorite wine?"

"Not a wine-for-the-rest-of-my-life, but I do prefer whites. You?"

"Beer."

She laughs, and it's such a better sound than the sobs.

A little later, I've polished off more cheese and crackers, along with some almonds and olives, and Arden has nibbled on a few strawberries and grapes.

"Let me walk you to your car," I tell her, after she packs up her basket. "Little red Honda down by the trailhead?"

"That's mine."

A few minutes later, I open the driver's side door

for her and then reach around to set the basket in the back seat.

I wag a finger at her. "Now, don't let him get you down, you promise me?"

She nods and smiles, but it's an apologetic one. "I'll do my best. And thank you, Gabe. You helped so much."

"I'm glad I was there. I'm glad my chest was there too, so you didn't knock any robins down with that sniper aim of yours."

She laughs then winces. "I'm sorry about that. Sorry you had to see me crying too."

"Don't think twice about it. Just promise me this: don't let any jerks win your heart again."

She holds up a pinky. "I promise."

I've never pinky sworn before, but now seems as good a time as any. I wrap my little finger around hers. "There. It's a deal. I'll be looking out for you."

"I appreciate that."

When she takes off, I turn around, pick up the pace, and resume my run, trying my best to think of other women. Like the cute little brunette from Whiskey Hollows I met the other night at a barbecue, or the leggy redhead from the gym who asked me to work out with her.

Anyone.

Anyone at all but the woman who's had her dignity stomped on.

The woman who is, for all intents and purposes, as unavailable as she was the day I met her.

The woman whose heart is broken over another man.

I shovel a hand through my hair as if I can rid myself of the inappropriate thoughts about how damn pretty she is, even with her tear-stained cheeks and sad brown eyes.

Pretty and technically available.

But I'd have to give myself the Jackass of the Century prize if I tried to take advantage of her right now, or anytime soon. And I'm not interested in collecting any trophies of that nature.

I run like my pants are on fire for five miles, and that does the trick.

For now.

* * *

After I leave the woods, I jog past my parents' home, dart up the stone path, and knock on the door. My dad answers quickly, clapping me on the back.

"Can't believe you didn't invite me to join you on your run," he deadpans. "I'm wounded."

"I'm only looking out for you. You'd get addicted if I did. You'd want to run marathons."

He ran plenty of marathons back in the day and kicked ass in every single one.

I walk past the living room, stopping to give my mom a kiss on the forehead as she reads some book she surely picked up from Arden's store.

Fuck. I wasn't supposed to be thinking of Arden.

In the kitchen I grab a glass of water, down a thirsty gulp, then set it on the counter as my dad strides in. "Want something to eat?"

"I already ate. Thanks."

"At Silver Phoenix Lake?"

I laugh. "Yeah. Funny thing. I ran into a picnic."

He arches one eyebrow in confusion.

I wave it off. "Long story."

"I have time."

"It's complicated."

He grabs a stool and sits down, folding his hands in his lap, waiting for me to tell him the tale.

I drag a hand through my sweaty hair. "So, Dad. There's this girl . . ."

3

ARDEN

One week later

When someone helps you, you thank that person.

That's simple good manners.

Perhaps it's a thoughtful card. Maybe it's a small gift. Sometimes it's baked goods.

By that same token, you should apologize properly when you inadvertently hit a person with a slice of cheese, even though I doubt Miss Manners has codified the protocol for that particular faux pas.

But I figured this one out on my own, since I pride myself on please, thank you, and proper apologies, as well as delivering them in the right fashion to the right people. If this makes me too nice, so be it. I will wear the "nice girl" sticker with pride.

Take that, David.

"Ha! There's nothing wrong with being nice," I

mutter as I put the finishing touches on the cookie-dough-stuffed pretzels I've just baked. This particular thank-you-for-the-shoulder-and-forgive-me-for-my-aim gift is taking the form of a sweet treat, since I bet they don't sell those cards at Hallmark.

And that's a good thing, since these pretzels smell sinfully good. So good, in fact, I bet they taste the way naughty feels.

Except I don't really know what that feels like, so I shove the thought out of my mind, grabbing a Tupperware container. Baked goods are most appropriate for a man you don't know that well. Sure, I've had plenty of conversations with Gabe prior to the Witness of My Tears Extravaganza. He joined the fire station a year or two ago, transferring from the city of San Francisco. Each time we've chatted, he's seemed both friendly and thoughtful, easy to talk to. But beyond the interactions when he visited my store to pick up new mystery novels or crossword puzzle books, or the times I ran into him at Vanessa's bowling alley, I don't know him terribly well.

Except I know he likes the ladies.

And the ladies like him.

If I were on the hunt for a one-night stand, or a real good time, he'd surely be the one I'd turn to. The man has charm for miles—a playboy with a heart of gold.

But I'm not going to thank him with my body. *Obviously.*

Food seems a close second on his list of favorite

things. Even if he was eating the picnic to be polite, he legit appeared to appreciate the spread. Men who work with their hands and bodies seem to dig gifts of fuel more than others.

Hence these kickass treats, courtesy of a recipe from my favorite Instagram baker, a fifteen-year-old in New York City who makes the most creative treats on her baking show. It's amazing what you can learn on Instagram once you look past the endless selfie sea. I press the green plastic top onto the container, sealing in the goodies with a pop. I wipe one palm against the other. *There.*

Tucking the treats into my shoulder bag, I leave my two-story yellow cottage with the wraparound porch I happen to think is the height of good living, lock the door, and walk six blocks to the town square where my very own bookstore sits proudly in the center of Oak Street. A New Chapter overlooks an expanse of emerald-green grass, park benches, and a statue of some old dude who founded this town in the gold rush era.

I open the cherry-red door to A New Chapter to a twin chorus of meows.

"Are you starving? Is that what you're telling me? Twelve hours is just too long for your bellies to handle?"

Henry and Clare answer with a duet of cat yeses, so I scoop some food for the rescue kitties the local shelter manager asked me to take in. How could I resist? They were homeless after the wine country fires last year, so I gave them four walls and a roof amidst the books, since customers dig bookstore cats. They purr their appreciation—a gratitude that will only last for a few minutes since they are, after all, cats.

When Henry's done, the big orange beast parks himself in the window for a public bathing, while Clare, the calico, lounges on a shelf in self-help today, watching every customer as if she's a guard cat, perhaps personally selecting the books for them. *That one needs more self-esteem.* She'll knock the right book off the shelf. *This one has mommy issues.* Clare will bat the ideal title with her paw, even if she's sprawled across the one slightly loose shelf.

I cruise through a busy morning, leading a story time for four-year-olds then helping some customers find the best coffee-table books to give as gifts.

As the clock ticks to noon, I grab my bag and find Madeline shelving books. I hired her a few months ago, and she's a go-getter—best employee ever.

"I need to run a quick errand. Can you handle the store?"

Her green eyes twinkle behind her red rhinestone-studded glasses. "Of course. Can I also work on the bestsellers display if no one's here?"

Boy, do I love go-getters. "Go for it."

I take off.

The guys usually wash the trucks now—a scheduling tidbit I only happen to know because of the number of times I've heard bookstore customers remark about the eye candy value of our local firemen—so this should be a good time to find Gabe. The firehouse is only a few blocks away, and as it comes into view, I spot Shaw and Gabe, who's dipping a cloth into a bucket and polishing the engine to a bright, gleaming shade of red.

My flats click-clack across the pavement. Gabe looks up and smiles at me, and for a brief moment, my chest flutters. The man is as handsome as a movie star. We're talking Hemsworth-brother handsome, which is about the best thing any man anywhere can look like. He wears dark pants and a blue T-shirt with the number of the firehouse on it: 212. He makes those clothes look better than a simple tee and slacks should, courtesy of a tall, hard, muscular frame with broad shoulders, strong biceps, and flat abs.

And I believe I'm ogling.

Maybe that's because there's just something about a fireman.

But I'm not here to admire him, or anyone, I remind myself. I'm here to be a gracious citizen of the town of Lucky Falls.

Look out, Gabe. The nice girl is coming for you.

4

ARDEN

I raise my chin, wanting him to see the confident side of me, rather than the snot-slipping-down-my-nose side. "Hey, Gabe. Just wanted to say thank you for helping me the other day. I have a little gift for you."

He drops the rag into a bucket, wipes his hands on a clean cloth, and strides across the driveway, out of earshot of the other guys. When he reaches me, he takes off his sunglasses, and those blue eyes . . . whoa. They're dreamier than I remembered. They're the color of the sky on a cloudless day, when all you want to do is soak up the rays.

"You didn't need to do anything," he says, and those baby blues—are they taking a quick stroll up and down my body?

Did he just do that?

There's no way he gave me a once-over.

I must be seeing things.

"Of course I did. You were amazing, and I appreciate it so much," I say, keeping my focus on my mission—*courtesy*—rather than on deciphering the hieroglyphics of men.

He waves a big hand dismissively. "I was happy to do it. Though, to be fair, the robins did seem quite pissed at me for running smack into their lunch plans."

I laugh. "Were they a little peeved or were they completely annoyed?"

"Oh, we're talking Angry Birds level," he says, and I crack up. "I suspect they were hoping to abscond with more of your picnic." He pats his belly, trim and flat. "Apparently, I'm now public enemy number one among the birds of Silver Phoenix Lake."

He's doing it again. Making every moment so damn easy—sweet and carefree, like his deep voice, his confident stride, his casual manner. "Is there a wanted poster up in the woods?"

"I believe there is. Those birds were raring to go—ready to fight me for the rest of those picnic goodies." He narrows his stare, intently serious. "Now, tell me, have you chucked any more crackers since then?"

I shake my head, smiling. "Nope. Not a single one."

"Hit any other joggers on the trail?"

"None at all. I'm going clean, I swear."

He offers a fist for bumping. "That's what I like

to hear. I'm glad you've had no need to turn snacks into projectile missiles. But you do know if you ever want to chuck something, you can call on me for target practice." He taps his chest. "I can handle it."

"Deal. And I'll try not to take you up on it." I dip my hand into my bag, taking out the Tupperware. "I made these for you this morning. Fresh out of the oven."

He lifts his nose and sniffs. "What have you got there? They smell like heaven."

"Just a little treat." As I give him the container, his fingers brush mine, lightly enough to deliver a little spark along my spine, like a low hum of possibility. "Cookie-dough-stuffed pretzels."

He whistles in appreciation. "Damn."

"You can share them with the guys. Even Shaw," I say, mentioning my best friend's brother, who works at this firehouse.

"I'll do no such thing. I don't believe in sharing." He says it almost flirtily, and I'm surprised at how much I like that tone. As much as I like the accidental brush of our fingers. Translation: more than I should.

But since I'm one week post breakup and still missing the good things about David, I'm pretty sure I shouldn't be liking anyone's tone or touch.

Note to self: find a pill that makes you immune to handsome men making flirty comments when you're still licking your wounds.

"Hey!" a familiar voice calls out. "You're not keeping those to yourself."

"Speak of the devil," I say as the dark-haired Shaw walks around the truck.

"I smell something good."

"I don't know what you're talking about." Gabe promptly stuffs the Tupperware under his shirt.

Shaw stops a few feet from me, lifting his chin. "Hey, Arden. What will it take for you to bring me some treats?" He waggles his eyebrows. "What did this fucker do to deserve some?"

No way am I going to tell Shaw—or anyone for that matter—how Gabe earned all the treats in the world, so I offer up another truth. "He bought a book from my store. Wait. Correction. Many books."

"Ah, so that's the trick. Maybe if I buy a tale or two sometime, you'll make me something tasty?"

Gabe claps him on the back, shaking his head. "You'd have to learn to read, then, Shaw. I know that'll be mighty tough for you."

"Just like two plus two is for you." Shaw flips him the bird as he returns to the other side of the truck.

Once Shaw is gone, Gabe frees the Tupperware from its hiding place. "I'll savor these, and maybe if I'm feeling generous, I'll dole some out to the guys. But that's highly unlikely since I'm a greedy bastard when it comes to delicious goodies. Which means I also ought to thank you for giving me new inspiration to run ten miles."

"Are you going to run off every single cookie-dough pretzel?" I ask, laughing.

"Every damn one. I believe in working out so I can both save lives and never ever have to count calories."

"That's because you can't count," Shaw shouts.

Gabe rolls his eyes, sets a hand on my back, and walks me down the sidewalk, farther away from the guys. He opens the Tupperware and takes a bite of a pretzel. He rolls his eyes and moans in pleasure, and the sound of his appreciation sends an unexpected shiver down my spine. Or perhaps it's not so unexpected, given how I reacted to the brief touch, then to his sexy tone.

"Holy shit. These are criminally good," Gabe says.

I beam. "I'm so glad you like them." Then I clear my throat and lower my voice so my next words are definitely only for us. Part of my thank you. "Also, if you ever need anything . . ." I say, and before it veers into coming-on-to-him territory, I pick up the pace, "like a book, or a crossword puzzle, or a wine recommendation, let me know." And that might still sound like a pickup line. He probably thinks I'm an emotional wreck anyway, so it's best to let him know I'm not trying to make a move. "As friends. If you need a friend."

My nerves somersault. I'm twenty-nine, and I just asked a guy to be friends with me. That's not normal, is it? That's either awkward or weird or . . . *nice*.

I shudder at the last one.

But Gabe seems to make everything look simple. He motions for me to come closer. "Do you like Words with Friends?"

A smile tugs at the corner of my lips. "Like gin loves tonic."

All the nerves fly away.

We exchange handles—MustLoveBooks for me, and CurveballorBust for him—and he thanks me once more for the treats, holding my gaze. "I think this could be the beginning of a beautiful friendship."

And that's exactly what it becomes over the next year, proving there's nothing at all wrong with being nice, since that's how we met—him being nice to me, and being nice in return.

Except I can't shake the feeling that being nice isn't all there is, especially when I start to feel I might like a little naughty.

5
GABE

One year later

"Your mom was here earlier. Let me see if Michael is ready for another visitor," the redheaded nurse tells me.

"Thanks, Darla," I say, and she gives me a flirty little sway of her hips as she heads down the hall of the assisted living home. I park myself in a leather chair in the fifth-floor lobby and return to the game on my phone.

I scan the board quickly, eyeing the possibilities. *R*. I tap my chin. Something with an *R*. Or a *C*. Or maybe . . .

I smile. Devilishly, I'm sure. Because I'm going to mess with Arden. Peering down the hallway, I see no sign of the nurse, so I open the chat with MustLoveBooks.

Gabe: Is R-A-B-E a word?

Arden: As in broccoli rabe? Yes. Whether it should be considered a food is debatable though.

Gabe: What in the holy hell is broccoli rabe? Why isn't it just broccoli? Why do we need to keep adding things to vegetables?

Arden: Don't you know? Vegetables now must be hipster hybrids of other vegetables. Also, rabe is the stalky, leafy part of the vegetable, if you want to get technical.

Gabe: You mean the part of the veggie that should go in the recycling bin?

Arden: Let me guess. You hate broccolini too.

Gabe: I'm not fooled by broccolini. If someone can't tell that word is a patent ruse to trick people into thinking broccoli is cute, they're a fool.

Arden: Obviously, you're no fool. You are a broccoli hater though. Now c'mon, play a word. A customer just walked in, and if my book-buying radar is still top-notch, I'm predicting he snags a hardback of the new Koontz.

Gabe: If you're right, bowling is on me.

As I planned all along, I form a word with my kickass bank of letters, and I swear I can hear her jaw dropping as I play — BROCCOLI.

Arden: You tricked me by building off my *C*!! I thought you were spelling RABE.

Gabe: Rabe is child's play. *blows on fingers*

Arden: And you used all your letters! You know I have to pay for bowling now. That trumps everything else.

Gabe: Oh, well, what do you know? I did play all my letters.

Arden: Also, the customer has the new Koontz tucked under his arm.

Gabe: Damn, you're sharp. But close is only good in horseshoes. Bowling's still on you.

I exit the app when the thunk of Darla's shoes

grows louder. She turns the corner and wiggles her fingers, giving me come-hither eyes, too, as she's done for the last few visits. "I'll take you to Suite 505 now."

Once I stand, she sets a hand on my arm, even though I know precisely where Suite 505 is since I've been visiting its resident as often as possible for a year now.

But Darla is persistent, and last time I checked, I was still single . . . ergo . . .

"My shift ends at five," she says.

"Good to know."

"And I don't have any plans tonight."

"Is that so?" I arch a brow.

She gives me the flirtiest smile in the history of smiles. "That is very much so."

I tell her to enter her number in my phone, and it takes less time than a peregrine falcon capturing a fish for her to type in those digits. I give her mine too.

"Text ya later." She spins on her heel and heads the other way.

I turn into Suite 505 and flash a smile to the man slouched in the blue upholstered chair, staring at the screen of the laptop perched on a bureau. I check out the action on the diamond. "Pops, are you watching last night's Giants game?"

"Yup. Posey hit a three-run homer."

But when I peer more closely at the screen, that's not Buster Posey running the bases. In fact, that's not who the Giants are playing this week. I'm pretty sure that's a game from last season.

"Pops, that looks like a game from last season," I say, gently trying to guide him back to the present.

He waves it off, tsking at the video. "You could have mowed him down with your curveball."

I laugh and clap him on the shoulder. "Doubtful, but glad you think so."

"I know so. I watched all your games."

That he did.

I settle in and enjoy the year-old game with him, catching up on things that happened yesterday and years ago, too, reminding him as best I can of what took place when.

* * *

Later that day, Darla texts me, asking if I want to get together.

I say yes, even though I'm wishing I could figure out the best way to broach the same subject with Arden.

Do you want to see a movie? Grab some dinner? Go to a beer festival? Drive to Calistoga and check out a bookstore there I know you'll love? Play mini golf over in Whiskey Hollows?

Those are all remarkably easy to say when asking someone out. Remarkably easy to say to Arden too.

Trouble is, when you become good mates with a

woman, it's hard to tell her that you think you might want more than just Words with Friends. You might want more than friends in general. Especially since I've never been known as the serious kind, and Arden most definitely isn't a casual girl.

That night I take out Darla. She's upbeat and fun, and a whole lot of flirty, but everything feels like a puzzle piece that doesn't quite fit.

I'm more distracted than I want to be on a date, and this is getting to be the norm for me.

And that's a problem.

6

GABE

Arden's busy with a customer, so I slip into her store unnoticed a few days later, and head straight for the mysteries. Pawing through the tomes, I find what I'm looking for.

The big orange beast.

If he's not parked in the window, he's often curled up by the newest titles. I suspect he likes the smell of the pages.

And yup, there he is, sprawled across a middle shelf, purring in front of the new Mary Higgins Clark. I reach for it, and the cat swats my arm. "Don't you want me to support your mistress's business?"

Henry twitches his tail, and clearly that means a big fat no.

I reach around him. He swipes at me again. "I think you might be bad for business if you keep that up."

He stretches, raises his furry chin, and shoots me a look of utter disdain before jumping off the shelves and sauntering haughtily away, tail high in the air.

I grab the novel. Tucking it under my arm, I make a beeline for the magazines and crossword puzzles, snagging a new book.

I peer around the corner, and Arden's back at the counter, head bent to study the computer screen, and damn does she look good today. Her blonde hair is piled high in one of those crazy buns. Whoever designed those buns should be given an award. On the surface, they shouldn't be attractive. It's a fucking bun, after all. But there's just something about that swept-up-and-still-a-little-messy look that revs my engine. Maybe it's the way that hairdo highlights her gorgeous cheekbones and accentuates lips that I know must be sinfully soft.

Or maybe it's that every little thing this woman does seems to get me going. That smile, her mind, her laughter . . . Truth is, I was thinking about Arden more than I was thinking about Darla on that date the other night. Thinking what it would take to have Arden sitting across from me at a restaurant as more than a buddy.

I head straight for the counter, plunking down the books with a thump. "You were busy, so Henry recommended these. Oh wait, he actually tried to attack me."

Arden startles then looks up and smiles. "Do you need me to get out my first aid kit and take care of all those terrible cat scratches he left on your arms?" She peers down. "Oh wait. You don't have any."

"I'm just saying. He's vicious."

"He's sweet."

I laugh. "We might have different definitions of the word 'sweet.'"

"We might indeed." She arches an eyebrow then slides me the books. "Your money's no good here. Take them."

I sigh. "No way. You can't do that."

She nods and gives a satisfied grin. "I can, and I will."

"Honestly, I'd like to pay. This one is for my mom and the other's for me."

Her smile shifts to one of curiosity. "Your mom's the one you buy the mysteries for?"

"You notice what I buy?"

"I do indeed. Maybe I'm a book spy."

"Well, 007, you've discovered my secret. I shop for my mom. She devours mysteries. She got that from her dad—my pops loves mysteries too. The more hard-boiled the better."

"The hard-boiled ones are a hoot. As for your mom, if she likes wine, tell her this Mary Higgins Clark pairs deliciously with a Bordeaux, since those wines are a little mysterious."

"I'll pass that on. She'll get a kick out of that."

"That's nice that you buy so many books for your mom."

"I told you that day at Silver Phoenix Lake—*nice*

is a good thing." I take out my wallet, fish around for a couple twenties, and set them on the counter.

"Gabe. Let me give these books to you."

I lean closer, shaking my head. "Let me support your business."

She screws up the corner of her lips, sighs, then holds up a finger. "Be right back."

A minute later she returns with a new hardcover. Glancing from side to side, she slides it over to me. "It's the new Sandra Brown. It doesn't come out for a few more days. Give it to your mom as a gift."

She gives me the change from the bills, and I thank her. "She'll love it."

And she does, indeed, when I head over for dinner and give the book to my mom.

"You win the prize for my best son ever," she says to me as she clutches the book.

"Was there anyone else in competition?" I tease, since I'm her only son.

"Hmm. You're right. But I still like you a whole helluva lot."

"Gee, thanks, Mom."

"I love you." She winks as she settles into the couch with her book then shoots me a genuine, "Thank you so much."

Later that night, there's a new game of Words with

Friends waiting for me, and the first word Arden has played is CURIOUS.

I want to read something into it, but mostly I'm damn impressed she led with a seven-letter word.

When my shift starts the next morning, we're called to a small warehouse fire, and handling that blaze is a hell of a lot easier than trying to use a word game to decipher a woman.

7

ARDEN

Men make no sense to me.

Like right now.

I'm on my turf, in my zone, recommending the right wine to go with the right book all night long like I'm a rock star at this, and I am. The whole time this guy keeps staring at me.

He's been here the last few nights, so I think he's a local.

He's handsome, with a square jaw and close-cropped brown hair. He wears a white dress shirt and a checkered tie, so I guess he's in banking or law.

Every night he buys a book, drums his fingers on the counter, and smiles before he asks me how I'm doing.

Every night I smile back and say, "Great."

Fine, I know I'm not like my friend Perri, smooth and cool when handling men. But she's a cop, and I'm a—well, I'm the good girl in the crew. Virgin till twenty. Serious boyfriend in college. Another serious boyfriend in my mid-twenties. Then David.

That's it. I've been with three guys. I've never played the pickup game. I've never even been on a dating app. And I've never made a move on a customer, even though Mr. Businessman has great taste. Last night he purchased Kristen Hannah's *The Nightingale*. The evening before it was *Hidden Figures*. Each time he asked me if I liked the books. *Of course*, I told him.

I mean, really.

They'd have to take away my license as a bookstore proprietor if I didn't adore those works.

Tonight, Mr. Businessman makes his way to the counter, a paperback tucked under his arm. There's a gray tie knotted on the cover, and I blink. Is that book what I think it is?

"Hey. How are you?" He grins at me a little sheepishly.

"Terrific. How are you?"

"Fantastic." He sets down the book, taps his finger against the knot, and meets my gaze. "I've heard so much about this book, I figured I should probably read it." He lowers his voice, glances from side to side. "But don't tell the guys at my office, 'kay?"

I bring my finger to my lips. "It'll be our little secret."

He smiles as I ring the purchase up. "Great. I figure it can't hurt to know what women want these days."

He's buying the book to better understand the fairer sex? Okay, I'm down with that, I suppose. "Smart man. A lot of women definitely still like reading this book."

"I'm sure I'll love it, then." He clears his throat and fixes his eyes straight on me. "Do *you* like it?" The words come out staccato. Like he truly wants to know what I think of *Fifty Shades of Grey*.

And this is why men make no sense.

Is he asking if I like being tied up? Does he want to know if I enjoyed the story? Is he asking my advice so he knows if it's a good gift for his girlfriend?

I answer truthfully. "It's a fun book. I can see why it was so popular."

My reply earns another smile. "Good to know."

I tuck the receipt between the pages. "Here you go."

He doesn't leave. "So, I've noticed you're here all the time. I trust this is your store?"

"My baby. Opened it five years ago. Love it, especially the book clubs."

"I like what you do here. It's more than just books that have people coming in."

Does he mean me? Or . . . "Well, I do work with book clubs all around the county and set up book and wine events—pairing wine with different books."

"That's awesome. Do you like wine?"

"Like a hammer loves a nail," I say, then I want to smack myself because does that sound like the worst come-on ever?

But he doesn't seem to notice. "There's a great wine bar down the street if you ever want to . . ."

I straighten my spine.

Holy smokes. He's asking me out. The handsome guy is asking me out.

Men do make some sense.

This computes.

But before I can say, *Why, yes, I'd love to*, I catch a final glimpse of the tie on the cover. Nerves grab hold of my throat. They tighten their grip, strangling words, choking them to silence. What if this guy is like David? What if he wants some version of a woman I don't know how to play? What if he's looking for a naughty girl rather than a nice one?

The nice girl in me answers, "Oh, that wine bar is great. You should totally go there."

I skedaddle to help another customer, nearly tripping over Clare, who gives me an imperious yellow-eyed stare for deigning to go near her.

"I froze. I completely froze. Like that dumb statue." I gesture to the dude riding the bronze horse as

Perri and I walk through the town square later that night.

"That is a seriously dumb statue. Want to topple it later?" she asks as she yanks her auburn hair into a tighter ponytail.

"Yes, let's deface public property. That'll help me get over my complete deer-in-the-headlights moment." I sigh and look at my good friend. "It gets better, right?"

She pats my shoulder. "I want to be totally sympathetic and tell you it's cool, no worries. But it's not going to get better unless you take a leap and get back in the game. That guy did a number on you."

I picture David's cutting words as he dropped me. "I know. And did I tell you that David is now engaged to the woman he started seeing after me? I can't even hate him for being a cad. He just didn't want me. He wanted her. They came into the store a week ago, and she was wearing a big fat ring."

Perri gives me a green-eyed sideways glance. "Sweetie, I'm not talking about David."

I stop at the edge of the square, furrowing my brow. "Who are you talking about, then?"

"Phillipe."

"Phillipe?"

She makes a rolling gesture with her hands. "Phillipe. French guy you dated for four years when he was living here. The sexy winemaker."

"I know who Phillipe is. I'm just not understanding the comparison."

"One-position Phillipe. He loved missionary more than anything in the world. Except his grapes."

I laugh. "Well, yeah. He was *absolutement* in love with his grapes."

"More important, Phillipe is kind of all you knew when it came to men. So when David said you were too sweet, it's only because you don't know if you like spicy."

We turn the corner, and I arch a brow. "That's the reason I froze in my store? Because I don't know if I like spicy sex?"

She nods. "Phillipe was pure vanilla."

For four years, Phillipe and I dated. He was wonderful—sweet and kind and a massive fan of being on top. In his defense, he was quite skilled at missionary, and we enjoyed the hell out of our horizontal time together. He reached all the spots he was supposed to reach including those starting with a G. But we never really ventured beyond that comfort zone, and the few times I asked, he never cared to mix it up.

I missed him only a little bit when he returned to Europe a few years ago to take over his family's vineyard in the Provence region.

"Your theory is I simply don't know what I might like in bed?" We wind our way toward our favorite bar.

"Exactly. Phillipe vastly preferred one way, and with David, you never had the chance to explore."

Wow. How did I not realize it before? But her

assessment is dead-on. Because of Phillipe I assumed most men liked sex the same way—on top, guy in charge, setting the pace. "I've only played it safe," I say, a little sad.

"You've only played it safe because it's all you've experienced. I'm not saying you have to take crazy risks. And there's nothing wrong with vanilla . . . unless you want chocolate or strawberry. Do you even know if you want chocolate or strawberry?"

I picture the artisan ice cream shop down the street. "Honestly, I kind of like that birthday cake with blueberry flavor at Salt and Straw."

Perri holds up her hands. "My point exactly. Have you ever had birthday cake with blueberry flavor in bed?"

I blink. "What would that even be?"

"Not missionary, that's all I know."

I laugh. "That's for sure. I tried to get Phillipe to mix it up. One time, I thought I would go all sexy on him. I took the initiative and dressed in come-hither lingerie—a white demi-cup bra and high-cut panties, and I climbed on top of him in bed when he was reading."

"And what did the missionary man do?"

I snort at the memory. "He said something sexy in French, and I was sure I was finally going to learn what it was like to be thrown down on the bed, to be yanked up on all fours. Hell, to have my ass smacked, and my hair pulled, and my panties ripped off."

"Uh. Yeah."

I shake my head as I recall what went down. "Instead, he tossed his book to the side, slid me underneath him, and made love to me, whispering sweet nothings in French the whole time."

"Boring. But the French dirty talk is a nice touch, so we can't dock him all the points."

"True. He deserves a minor commendation for his ability to say swoony things, like *je te veux tellement*. But being taken would have been better, right?"

"*Mais oui.*" Perri laughs. "I can absolutely confirm that being taken is often better than being talked to. Give me a strong, silent, tatted-up man on a motorcycle who throws me down on the couch, and all he has to do is grunt, *Fuck. Now.*"

"A caveman is all you require?"

She shrugs in a way that conveys her answer. "Pretty much."

I pat her shoulder. "I'll be on the lookout for you."

"And what about you? What do *you* want?"

I let her question marinate, trying to figure out what I'm missing. "I don't need to be Christian Grey's plaything, and I don't want to be tied up in the Red Room. But that's what stung about David's parting words. He never gave me the chance." I flash back to that day at Silver Phoenix Lake, but further too, back to all the days with him. "Though, honestly, I never took the chance either. I never asked for anything else. And I honestly wouldn't mind finding out if other positions are how they make them out to be in books."

"I bet Mr. Businessman would have helped you find out."

I sigh. "Now I'll never know what Mr. Businessman really wants, or if he likes birthday cake sex."

She nudges me. "Also, seriously. How did you miss the signs? The dude bought *Hidden Figures* and *The Nightingale* and asked your opinion on them, and you didn't realize he was asking you out?"

I offer up a lame, "He might have been buying them for a girlfriend."

"And tonight you learned he was buying them as conversational lubricant to talk to you."

We reach our favorite bar and head inside, where I order a white wine and she asks for a beer.

She taps the bar. "I think it's time to find out if you have a little Ana in you."

"Whoa. I am not submissive."

"Hello! I meant the sexy elevator kiss. It's time to find out if you'd like being kissed hard in an elevator."

My body tingles with the memory of that scene. The way he grabbed her wrists. Pinned them above her head. He *took* her kiss. "Yes, please. I'll have one hot, sexy elevator kiss to go. Trouble is, how do I get it? You're bold enough to ask out guys you like. How do you do it?"

"I'm naturally a big mouth. But bear in mind, there's a flip side. A lot of guys think because I have a badge and a uniform, that means I want to lock them up and throw away the key, or be smacked with a billy club."

"But don't you just *love* all that?"

"I like other things, and I often ask for it. My point is this." She tips her beer bottle in my direction. "The next time a hottie in your bookstore asks you out, say yes. It's that simple."

But is it? Is it truly that simple? I wish I could feel as comfortable with other guys as I do with Gabe. Maybe then I'd have a clue what they want.

8

ARDEN

Bullseye.

Look at that. I can rock a dartboard like nobody's business. It's so much easier than saying yes to a date with a guy and having my sexual prowess, or lack thereof, labeled as vanilla once again.

"And on that note, looks like I'm in line to take home the winner's trophy tonight," I say to Gabe.

He arches a brow. "Oh, do we have trophies? Where are they? I didn't see any when I walked in." He scans the tables and the bar in the game room at the Pin-Up Lanes.

"I ordered some. They're on the way over." I strut past him, feeling confident about my chances to win at darts tonight. I tap my index finger to my tongue and touch the air, making a sizzling sound. I don't freeze up at darts. Nice girls can play darts, evidently.

He chuckles, shaking his head. "East, you've got another think coming."

I straighten my spine as he raises his arm. "Wait. You said 'think.'"

"I did. Now, I know this is your trick to try to knock me off my game, so move along, honey. Move along." He tries to shoo me away from him.

"No one says that. It's like *intents and purposes*. Almost everyone thinks the phrase is 'intensive purposes' when it's *intents and purposes*."

"Or *stock and trade* when it's *stock-in-trade*. Don't be so surprised that I understand etymology. I've got beauty and brains." He taps his skull, flashing me an over-the-top smile.

"I just hardly ever hear anyone say *You've got another think coming*."

"I can say *another thing coming* if you want," he says in a sexy drawl.

One I like more than I should.

I laugh to dispel the effects I'm feeling from the elixir of pleasure that is his hot, husky voice. "You know how I feel about words. I like when they're used correctly."

"I do indeed know that about you." The fact is, Gabe knows a lot about me. It's funny, or maybe not so funny, how someone seeing you at your worst can forge an instant friendship and a tight-knit bond. That's exactly what happened with us.

"Hey, did your mom like the Sandra Brown?"

"Loved it. She also said she felt like a little scofflaw, reading it early."

I place my index finger on my lips. "Shh. Don't tell the book's publisher, or I will be in some kind of hot water."

"Oh, so I have leverage over you now. What are you going to do to ensure I protect your secrets?"

"Bribe you by keeping Mama Harrison in top secret, embargoed copies of popular books that I *only* give early to her?"

He furrows his brow like he's considering this, then extends his free hand. "Deal." Then he shoos me off. "Now stop trying to distract me. You're terrible at it anyway. You're also not the only one with impeccable aim." He raises his arm above his head and narrows his eyes. He cocks his arm, his eyes lasering on the target. For a moment, I let myself enjoy the view.

I mean, I am great friends with a hottie.

Gabe is crazily handsome in a how-is-it-possible-to-be-that-good-looking way. His blue eyes are the kind to get lost in and his arms are ideal to wrap around and comfort you.

I don't know the nitty-gritty of his dating life, but he's rarely without female companionship. A few weeks ago, he took out the woman who cut his hair. I bet she was bold enough not to botch a date request. And I bet I could ask him for tips on what men really want. Perhaps we could sit down, I could take some notes, and I'd be good to go. Ready for the next Mr. Businessman situation before it goes belly-up.

His dart makes a beeline for the target but misses. I thrust my arms in the air in victory. "I've still got it."

He offers a hand for high-fiving, and I smack back. "Pizza is on me," Gabe says.

"Is it a pizza night?"

"Of course."

"Oh, right. You're having a long-standing love affair with pizza."

He laughs. "See, Arden? You know me so well."

And I do. I know what Gabe wants. He's easy to understand. If only I could apply these friendship skills to the dating game. If I could take the ease I have with him and transfer it to dating, I'd feel . . . empowered.

I let that word roll around in my head, and it hits me. *Empowered* is exactly what I want to feel.

As we head to the bar in the bowling alley to order a cheese pie, my friend Vanessa stops by our table, her dark-brown locks curled up at the ends, '50s-style, just like her bowling alley. The entire place is a throwback to the *Happy Days* life, complete with vintage posters and a retro theme. Makes sense, since she's always been the queen of vintage. Tonight, she wears a red-and-white gingham skirt and a white cap-sleeved retro blouse.

"Are you playing waitress this evening?" I tease,

since I know she's the chief cook and bottle—and bowling ball—washer when she needs to be.

"I do it all. But mostly I want to remind you two to come to the fundraiser this weekend."

Gabe laughs. "As if I'd miss it. I'll be here with the guys." He points to me. "And you and I have some games to play, so you better save some lane time for me."

"Count on it."

See? Saying yes to Gabe is easy because he's a friend. Friends are easy to understand.

And because we're friends, I'm starting to formulate a plan. It's the seed of an idea now, but I'll spend time with it, tweak it, refine it.

After we eat our pizza, he asks if I'm up for a game of bowling.

I say yes. It's good practice, after all, and I need time to devise my plan.

I need to practice saying yes when I want to, and I intend to do precisely that.

9
GABE

I've been called many things.

Pain in the ass, by my sister.

Top prospect, by the major leagues.

Playboy, charmer, and ladies' man, and any and every combination of those.

I'm not saying any of those terms are wrong.

But I do have to wonder what the hell is wrong with being a ladies' man?

Women are basically the best thing ever. They're beautiful, lovely, witty, clever, and a whole hell of a lot of fun to spend time with.

Women are my favorite gender.

My best friend in high school was Lacey Cunningham, a soccer star. In college I was tight with Vivian Wells, who was a goddess at grammar. And now, here I am with Arden. She is fit as a fox in that plaid skirt and matching red tank top, and I want to ask why the hell she likes to bowl in a skirt, but I also don't want her to ever consider bowling in anything but a skirt.

"So how was the hair stylist?" she asks, inquiring about a date from a few weeks, maybe a month ago.

"It was fine."

"Fine?"

"Yes. Fine." I grab a green ball.

"Fine is not an answer," she says, egging me on. "Are you seeing her again?"

"She was a lovely lady, but there was no, how shall we say, *spark*."

She pouts playfully. "Poor Gabe. No spark must have made you so lonely."

"Oh, I didn't say I was lonely."

She swats me. "You're such a pig."

I oink.

"But why would you sleep with her if there was no spark?"

"Oh, there was a physical spark. She's a fiery one."

"So she was naughty?" Arden asks carefully, as if she's measuring her words.

"Maybe a little, but there's nothing wrong with that."

Arden nods, humming. "Nope. Nothing wrong with that at all. *How* was she naughty though?"

The question comes out like she's asking it in class, and her tone makes me laugh. "Are you taking notes?"

"Yes. I'm working on a report for the town bulletin." Her tone is 100 percent deadpan.

"I don't want to kiss and tell, and definitely not for the same bulletin where Pedro Hardaway advertises his plumbing services and Sally Caruso offers dog sitting by the hour. So stop using your superior powers of persuasion to try to get me to give up all sorts of details, and get focused on your game, woman. I want to beat you." I head to the lane and take my first shot, sending the ball straight to the finish line.

"Did she have a riding crop and ask you to hit her with it?" Arden asks as the ball slams into eight pins.

It's a damn good thing I wasn't throwing the ball when she asked that because it might have landed five lanes over.

Cracking up, I head over to the ball return. "That's a little specific and definitely inappropriate for a town bulletin."

"Did she like to be tied up?"

I shake my head. "Not going to go there."

When the green ball pops up, I palm it then slide my fingers in the holes. She follows my hand with her eyes. "Do you mean she likes to be . . . filled in all the holes?"

I laugh so hard I nearly choke. "Who has the naughty mind tonight? I was simply getting ready to throw a spare."

She doesn't even blush. She's undeterred. "Did she ask you out on the date?"

I frown, trying to remember who asked first. I shrug. "I honestly don't recall."

"You're not helpful. You won't answer my questions, and you won't tell me how it started."

"That's partly because it's not going to continue. I'm not seeing her again." I return to the lane and send the ball down the hardwood, waiting until it smacks the remaining two pins, nailing the spare. When I turn around, I ask, "Why do you want to know so badly what it was like?"

Arden has never pumped me for dating details before. Not the tawdry ones at least. I half want to believe it means something, but it could mean nothing at all.

"Just curious," she says nonchalantly as she grabs her favorite purple ball. She makes it sound so casual, her inquiry. But there's that word again from Words with Friends—*curious*—and it snags on my brain. Why exactly is she so curious?

A second later, she gives me the answer. "Everyone's coming into the bookstore buying these racier books. It just got me thinking."

She turns away, heads to the top of the lane, and holds the ball in front of her.

And her comment has me thinking too.

About dirtier books.

If she reads them.

What she likes between the sheets.

What her curiosity has piqued exactly. Well, besides *me*. I'm definitely piqued, and I make a quick adjustment in my jeans so it's not so damn obvious.

As she tosses the ball down the lane, her left leg arcing behind her, showing a hint of the back of her thighs, I groan.

I want to know the landscape of her body. Want to slide my hands up and down her legs, nibble on her ass, and make her whimper.

I would love to know what would make Arden go wild in bed.

That's not only because I'm wildly attracted to her.

It's because I want to know what makes her tick in the bedroom as well as I know what excites her out of it.

I want to know her in every way.

Sooner or later, I'm going to have to figure out how to drive this car clear out of the friend zone.

Sooner is my preference.

Like maybe this weekend at the party here at the bowling alley.

Maybe I can find a way to pique her interest in me.

10

ARDEN

"What kind of wine would you say goes well with a memoir? Something really hard-hitting and designed to rip my heart out?"

The question comes from a bespectacled woman who's pawing through my display of non-fiction bestsellers.

"Like *Educated* by Tara Westover?"

"Yes. Exactly."

I tap my chin. This is my forte. "You definitely want a merlot. It's bold and powerful, but the best ones with the most fantastic grapes are so good, they make you want to cry."

"Like *Educated*." Her lips curve into a grin, her laugh lines a happy pair of parentheses.

"Exactly. Want me to set everything up for your book club?"

"Yes. It's going to be a raucous night of…"

"Drinking wine and only very occasionally discussing books?"

"That's exactly what a good book club should be." The woman extends a hand. "I'm Miriam."

"Arden East."

"Someone likes you very much to give you that name."

"My mom is pretty rad," I say, thinking of my parents, who are happily traveling the world in their much-deserved retirement. This month they're in Australia and sent me an email about their visit to the Sydney Opera House. *"It's better than all the travel books say,"* my mom told me.

Miriam points to the nook in the back of the store, reserved for book clubs. "Is tomorrow night available? We plan on being loud and a little obnoxious."

"As if I would want you to be anything else," I tell her with a smile. "The store closes at eight on book club nights with my rowdiest gals. Would that work for a starting time?"

Miriam's blue eyes sparkle with a yes.

The next evening, she parades in a troop of women about twice my age and introduces me to CarolAnn, who wears her jet-black hair in a sexy, messy bun; to Sara, sporting cat-eye glasses and skinny jeans; and to hobo-chic-styled Allison, who tells me I'm beautiful.

Possibly, I fall in love with all of them on first sight.

I busy myself with placing orders on the store computer at the front while the ladies discuss *Educated* and drink a rich merlot from Oak Hollows Vineyard, a few miles south of us. But soon enough, the wine loosens lips, and the conversation shifts.

They're no longer discussing a young girl raised in a survivalist family. They've sidestepped from the author's first boyfriend to their own first loves. They then jump seamlessly to current lovers, husbands, and beaus.

As I let my distributor know I need twenty more of the new Nora Roberts romance, I hear that black-haired CarolAnn still likes it doggie-style at age sixty.

While checking on my shipment of quirky travel guides, I learn that hobo-chic Allison wants to explore clamps.

As I hit the order button on a new clean recipe book, I discover that skinny-jean-wearing Sara and her younger boyfriend like to park at the end of a deserted road so she can give him a blow job in the car. Sometimes, if Sara's really frisky, her boyfriend will pull her hair and spank her.

During the blow job.

An unexpected pang of envy stabs me right in the solar plexus.

I want to know what that's like. All of it—the blow job in the car, the spankings, the ease with which she talks about it. Most of all, I want to know how the hell studious-looking Sara has navigated the path to car spankings.

I step away from the desk and straighten some shelves, doing my best to pretend I'm not eavesdropping as I pick up a "You Can Have It All" style of self-help guide that I'm positive Clare knocked over earlier.

"Look, I know these aren't crazy kinky things, but I feel like I've been liberated since Chuck left me and I met my new boyfriend," Sara says, in a husky, Kathleen Turner-esque tone. "Chuck was the same old, same old. But Javier? No way. He's a different creature entirely, and it's freeing. Do you know what I mean?"

"Absolutely. You're sexy and single and you have a hot man who wants you. There's no reason you shouldn't do exactly what you want to do," CarolAnn adds, almost like she's giving a *you go, girl* speech. Which she kind of is.

"How did you get Javier to pull your hair? Was it his idea or yours?" Allison asks, and I don't want to tune out a second of this conversation even though it's making me keenly aware of my lack of an interesting sex life.

I've never been spanked.

I've never bitten.

I have never given a blow job in a vehicle.

I used to think I was simply a good girl. I boxed myself into a category—I'm the safe one, I'm the one who likes beds.

And I do like beds.

But what if I like cars more?

With a deep, needy ache, I desperately want to know what I'm missing.

"Easy," Sara declares, then details precisely how she accomplished the hair-pulling and spanking. I take furious mental notes, adding the ideas to my burgeoning plan.

If the sixty-something ladies in this book club are sowing their wild oats, it's time for me to damn well do it.

I resolve to make a change.

Tomorrow night I'll see Gabe at the bowling alley for the party. I intend to walk out of there with a solid plan to figure out what's been missing all these years.

When the ladies leave, I say good night, lock the door, and grab a stack of how-to books. After a few hours of study, I make a list. Books rule. Research rocks.

By the time the clock chimes midnight, I have one hell of a plan.

I am woman. Hear me roar.

11
GABE

"And I believe we set a record today." Shaw stretches his neck, cracking it loudly as he slams his locker shut next to the baby-faced Charlie, one of the paramedics who works frequently with us.

"For the number of non-fatal medical emergencies?" I put the rest of my gear away at the end of our twenty-four-hour shift, which is thankfully, finally fucking over. Felt like a forty-eight-hour one. But with only minor injuries and no deaths or losses of limb, I'll chalk it up to a damn good shift.

Shaw shakes his head. "No. For no phone numbers given out."

Charlie drags a hand through his dark hair. "It's a record shift of epic failures in that department."

I roll my eyes. "You two clowns do know it's called work? That thing we do all day long?"

"Huh." Shaw scratches his unshaven jaw,

affecting surprise. "Is that the name of it? Did you know that, Charlie?"

The younger man feigns shock. "I had no idea."

I point to the two of them. "Well, I'm glad to finally be the one to inform you, since you seem to be under the impression that it's a pickup market."

"Oh yes. That's exactly what I was thinking when we responded to a shortness of breath call for the eighty-year-old Mrs. Miller," Shaw remarks.

I give my buddy a sharp-eyed stare. "I don't think it's the eighty-year-old Mrs. Miller's phone number that you were angling for." I crack up as it hits me. The woman's twenty-something granddaughter was the one who made the call and then seemed unable to look anywhere but at Shaw as he took grandma's vitals. The trim, toned blonde ogled him the whole time, and I was positive Shaw would be shacking up with her tonight, but it sounds like nothing came of it. "You didn't get the girl's number?"

Shaw shakes his head.

And that means I need to give him hell. "You're losing your touch, man. You need to retire and live life as a monk."

He lets his head hang, forlorn. "I know. What is wrong with me?"

"Everything," Charlie says in mock seriousness. "Do you need me to give you some lessons on how to win the ladies? Everyone knows paramedics have better game than firemen."

I clap Shaw on the back. "You couldn't close the deal. Clearly, it's time to accept you're an ugly, old bastard and you have *zero* game."

"Same as you."

"Of course. I'm hideous. I also need to jet."

Charlie lifts a hand to wave. "I need to deal with some paperwork. See you guys later."

"Catch you next time," I say as Shaw and I take off.

"Speaking of closing the deal," Shaw says as we leave the firehouse and head down the street, "are you ever going to close the deal with Arden?"

I stop in my tracks, bristling at the mention of the woman I very much want. I narrow my eyes. "What are you talking about?"

He sets a hand on his stomach, laughing. "Do you actually think I don't know that you have it bad for her?"

As a matter of fact, I was hoping so.

"I don't have it bad," I deny, even though he's as right as the Earth rotating around the sun.

"You can lie to yourself, buddy. But I'm not fooled. You should do something about it."

I sigh as we turn the corner. I could keep up the ruse, but he's already seen through me. What's the point in pretending? "Fine. Fine. You win."

He pumps a fist. "Called it. Even though it was patently fucking obvious, Twenty-Three," he says, using his nickname for me, my number when I played pro ball.

"Like wearing-a-billboard obvious?"

He nods several times. "But that's because I know your style. Maybe it's not obvious to her. Which brings me back to closing the deal. Are you or aren't you going to let the woman know you have a thing for her?"

I drag a hand through my hair. "I'd like to. But then what if it goes south?"

"South? The direction most relationships go?"

I laugh mirthlessly. "Yes. Isn't that the truth?"

"Sure seems to be."

"Hell, I went out with a woman who works at the retirement home, and now I get the cold shoulder from her when I go to visit my pops. I was a gentleman too. I made my intentions clear from the start. Nothing serious. But she wanted more, and now she scowls at me."

"You can withstand a scowl, surely?"

"Yeah, I can handle scowls." I take a deep breath. "But I don't want Arden to scowl, you get me?"

Shaw nods, and we stop at his blue pickup truck, parked near the station. "I hear ya. Some women are special. You don't want that to happen with your bowling buddy. But look at what happened to your major league career. You went for it, and you had no regrets, Twenty-Three."

I was recruited out of college by the Texas Rangers and played minor league ball for three seasons with that organization. A relief pitcher with a killer curveball, I was called up to the majors and played there for one glorious season before my shoulder fried like a circuit board left in the sun.

Retirement came swift and early, but I didn't let it get me down. I had choices. I'd parked all my major league money in a mutual fund so I could let it grow. I had no interest in lamenting what didn't happen. I wasn't going to be that guy clinging to one great year and never moving on. I've seen *Eastbound and Down*, thank you very much. And while Danny McBride is funny as fuck, there was no way I would become a washed-up baller clawing my way back to the pitcher's mound. Instead, I moved on, since the world only spins forward.

When I was a kid and my pops asked me what I wanted to be when I grew up, I always had two answers—ballplayer and a fireman.

I always wanted both.

I'd done all I could on the first one, saved some good money from that year in the show, and it was time to head into career number two.

I've had no regrets—I've loved being a firefighter just as much.

Don't look back.

Take your chances.

Go for it.

I need to fucking go for it with Arden, even if it means blowing out my shoulder.

The trouble is, in this analogy the shoulder is our

friendship, and I honestly don't want to see it blow up.

But that's the chance I have to take.

She's the woman I can't get out of my head.

She's no Darla. She's no hairstylist. She's the one I want for more than a one-and-done date. I want more than a casual thing with her.

I want all in.

*** * * ***

"Pops, when you met Nana, did you know right away you wanted to take her out?"

My grandpa scrunches his forehead like it hurts him to think. In some ways, I suppose it does.

"I knew I wanted her to type memos for me," he says, then winks, and that makes me happy, his awareness.

I laugh, patting his arm. "You old fox, falling for your secretary."

He shrugs as if to say *what can you do?* "Emily could write memos like nobody's business, Gabe."

I smile, loving days like today when he's here, fully present, remembering. "So you went for it?"

"Do I look like a fool?"

"No, sir. You do not."

Nor do I want to look like one.

Tonight, I resolve to bowl a game with the guys like I promised, find a way to get Arden the hell out of the bowling alley, and let her know I want to take her out.

Again and again.

When I exit Pops's suite, I glance down the hall, peering left and right. I breathe a sigh of relief when I don't see Darla.

But that's stupid.

It's not like she's going to ambush me with tears or rage. Hell, we went on one date. That was all. Sure, she wanted another and said as much, but I wasn't feeling it, so I said thanks but no thanks.

I have to deal with running into her, if it happens.

And when I reach the main floor, it does. She's turning the corner, heading straight toward me.

She lifts her chin proudly. "Hello, Gabe."

"Hello, Darla."

She walks past me, looking straight ahead with a cold, stony-faced, I-don't-even-notice-you stare, and I make my way to the parking lot, ready to move on. No more ladies' man.

I'd like to be a one-woman man.

12

ARDEN

I survey the scene at Pin-Up Lanes. Retro tunes play overhead, and a stream of people smile and toast, having a good time.

My friend Finley from the next town over is here, and she and her new guy Tom are bowling. I stroll by her lane, tapping her on the shoulder after she finishes her turn.

"Hey, you. How's your show going?" Finley's a TV comedy writer.

"I have more than one hundred viewers, so I'd say it's going better than my last show," she says, her light blue eyes twinkling.

"Oh, please. I'm sure you had more than that."

"I wouldn't be too sure about that," she says dryly.

"Well, I'm glad the new one is doing better then." I tip my forehead in Tom's direction. "And how's the new man?"

Her grin is infectious. "He makes me laugh and he makes me happy. And, well, I kind of can't take my hands off him."

I smile. "I suppose that's how it should be."

"I'm a big advocate of wanting to get your hands on the man you like."

We catch up briefly on her life, when Tom comes over after taking his turn. He pecks a kiss on her cheek and says hello.

"You guys look like you're having fun, so I'll let you keep it up."

I wander past the crowds, and find Vanessa at the bar.

"I'd say your Celebrate Summer Party is a huge hit," I tell Vanessa from my perch at the bar, as I scan the crowd for Gabe. My purse is in Vanessa's back room. My list is tucked safely inside a book in the bag. My plan is solid.

"Thank you. I'm pretty damn proud of this event, myself. Can't believe I pulled it off."

"I can. You're kickass at everything you do. Do I need to remind you of how we used to wander past this bowling alley when it was that dilapidated, lamely named 'County Lanes'? It smelled like bacon grease and half the lanes were broken, and you said, 'I'm going to fix that up and add some style.'"

Vanessa laughs, and I swear the memory of her determined teenage self flickers in her eyes. "I loved bowling and retro clothes as a kid. I guess it just worked out."

"It didn't *just work out*. You made it happen."

She lifts a glass and toasts. "To us. The Kickass Girls of Lucky Falls," she says, using the name we bestowed on our trio when we were younger. "Well, minus one, but Perri's surely out kicking ass and taking names."

"And she's doing that literally," I say, raising my Riesling and clinking it to Vanessa's water glass.

I take a drink of the crisp wine. I've deemed it the ideal pairing for going out on a limb. It's fresh and bright, with an effervescent aftertaste. It's ready to show off its flavors.

I'm ready too.

Tonight is a perfect night for a proposal. Gabe has finished his shift, he's relaxed, and we've already planned to play a game or two here at the event. The Celebrate Summer fundraiser benefits the first responders in the county—the police, firefighters, and paramedics who have been tasked with harder than normal work thanks to the fires that raged for days in vineyards and across once lush, rolling green hills. That's why the bowling alley, complete with karaoke bar, darts, pool tables, and twenty lanes, is stuffed to the gills. The first responders here have earned so much well-deserved support.

"You can't beat the view tonight," Vanessa says, her eyes drifting over the crowd and finding the pack of men from the station at lane twenty, including Gabe, Jackson, Charlie, and Perri's brother, Shaw. Vanessa's gaze lingers on Shaw for a beat longer than usual. Maybe two beats longer, come to think of it.

I shoot her a curious stare. "Are you checking out the Shaw view?"

She scoffs then grabs a glass of water and downs a gulp. "No way. I was just talking about all of them. They're all the reason fireman calendars and fireman fantasies exist, right?"

I decide to let the Shaw issue go for tonight — I don't need to give her the inquisition on a stare that lasted a little longer than usual. "We do seem to possess an embarrassment of riches in the hot fireman department. I bet Guinness World Records would like to know what we've accomplished in our little town."

She wiggles her dark eyebrows and motions for me to inch closer as the music shifts to Elvis Presley. "Want to know why we have so many hotties here?" She drops her voice to a whisper. "I planted seeds. Hot fireman seeds."

"And now they grow from the fields," I say, laughing, as Gabe raises a hand from across the alley and waves at me.

My stomach flips.

Stupid stomach.

It's just a wave.

Why the hell is my stomach flipping?

I wave back, rehearsing the words that I want to say to him later. I've mapped it all out.

So I have this idea . . .

I'd like to ask for your help . . .
How would you feel about doing . . . ?

Vanessa drums her fingers on the bar. "And now I can ask you the same question. Are you checking out the view of Gabe? Looks like you're giving him a very thorough undressing right now."

I snap my gaze away from the hottie. I mean, my friend. *My friend.* Only my friend. "I am not disrobing him."

Vanessa rolls her brown eyes. "You kill me, girl. I love how you deny it." She raises her pitch, imitating me, evidently. "*Oh, we're just friends. Oh, he's my bowling partner.*" She snorts and goes back to her own voice. "More like the man you've been hanging out with for the last year, secretly staring at and imagining naked the whole time."

"I do not secretly stare at him." Sure, Gabe is so handsome it's nearly criminal, and admittedly, I have experienced a fair share of tingles and shivers when he's accidentally touched me. But our friendship is what matters most.

"True. You don't secretly stare. You stare at him in public."

"I don't do that at all. I'm simply attentive. To all my friends."

She snorts. "That's a good one."

"But it's true," I say, perhaps to remind myself of my plan.

I'm going to ask him for help as a friend, and only as a friend. I made a promise to myself the day

David ditched me—no more dalliances with unworthy men. Not that Gabe is unworthy, but he does like the ladies, and I don't want to be someone's "nice" comparison point ever again. But I very much want to know what naughty things I might like, and I want to learn that without making a fool of myself when I have no idea what goes where in what position, or even what to say to get myself in that position in the first place. But I haven't asked Gabe yet, so I don't want to say a word to anyone else.

Besides, there's nothing to share. This is only a little exercise between pals. "Just because we hang out doesn't mean we're going to do anything more. A man and a woman can be friends, thank you very much."

Vanessa sets her glass on the bar. "You might see it that way, but he's always looking at you like he wants you."

I startle at her comment, my skin buzzing, betraying my brain. But I keep my focus tight. There is no room for a Gabe attraction in my life. None at all. "You're crazy. He doesn't look at me like that."

"You're crazy, because yes, he does."

I shake my head, wishing the idea didn't delight some part of me. "We're friends. It's not like that."

"That's why your cheeks are all red and flushed."

I raise a hand to touch my cheek. Maybe it's a little warm in here. "I can be friends with a good-looking man and not jump his bones."

"If you insist." She nods toward the other side of the bar. "I need to go check on the patrons."

"Do you mind if I pop into your back room?" I ask. "I need to have a private conversation with someone."

She arches a curious brow. "And who would that be?"

"Don't worry about it," I say, trying to be light.

Vanessa crosses her arms. "No. You can't borrow my back room."

"Oh, c'mon. Why not?"

"Because friends don't keep secrets about who they're hosting private meetings with in other friends' back rooms."

"Fine." I sigh. "It's Gabe. Okay?"

She smirks, giving me the most knowing smile she's ever given me. "Are you going to plant hot fireman seeds with him?"

I decide to deflect with wordplay. "If anyone would be planting seeds, I'd think it'd be him."

Her jaw drops.

"But the answer is no. I just need to talk to him about something. I'll update you later."

She shoots me a sharp stare. "You better. Use of my back room includes giving me a detailed briefing."

"I promise."

"Then my back room is your back room."

13

ARDEN

I finish my go-out-on-a-limb Riesling, and when Gabe is done with his frame, he strides over and parks himself on the stool next to mine. My stomach flip-flops, and my palms are clammy. I need to make my request soon, otherwise it'll nag at me all night.

"Hey, East. What's cooking? Did you save a game for me?"

"Always." But I don't want to play a game right now. I want to make my pitch, and I don't want to wait another second. I've been saying the words in my head all day. "But first, do you have a second to chat privately?"

Worry creases his brow. "Sure. Everything okay?"

"Absolutely." I smile, keeping the mood light and easy, or so I hope.

We head to the back room, where filing cabinets line the walls next to a desk stacked with papers.

Across from us is a green leather couch. I don't sit. I don't want to delay. I swallow, steeling myself as I find my courage and screw it to the sticking point. Like the ladies in the book club. *Ask for what you want.*

I reach into my bag, take out a book, and show it to him. Though I read several the other night, this one is the closest to what I want.

Fifty Ways to Spice Up Your Love Life.

"Is this for me?" His expression is curious, lips quirked up in a question.

My throat is dry. I shake my head. "It's for me."

Confusion flickers across his blue eyes. "Okayyyyy."

I grip the book hard. "I have this idea that I want to try some spices."

"Are you seeing someone you want to get spicy with?" It sounds like the words taste like bitter paprika to him.

"No." This is harder than I thought. Because of what Vanessa said. Because Gabe is so handsome, so kind, so easy that a part of me keeps thinking how much I want to try all these things with him. To feel what might come next after the little shivers up my spine.

Only that's not what I'm asking.

I don't want a typical hands-on lesson in seduction. Please. That'd ruin our friendship, and our friendship means the world to me. I simply won't risk it.

But we don't need to get naked for me to learn. You don't practice CPR on a real person. You do it on a dummy. We don't need to walk the walk.

He can spank me with my jeans on.

He can pull my hair on my front porch.

He can bite my neck without it leading to anything more than information.

Intel.

That way we stay friends.

Besides, he's not playing the same long game I am. He's a short-term guy, and I respect that, but I'm a long-term kind of woman.

I dig down deep. "I'd like to ask for your help." Taking a breath, I pause before I lay it all on the line. "I'm not terribly experienced in the bedroom, but I'm incredibly curious, and I'd really like to know if being tied up, taken over the back of the sofa, stopping for an impromptu hookup while out for a drive, making out in an elevator, or having my hair pulled so hard I see stars is my cup of tea. How would you feel about doing some research with me? Say, over the next week?"

14

GABE

Come again?

Did she say what I think she said?

As in, the answer to all my prayers?

I have half a mind to punch the sky and do a victory strut.

But one, I'm not an asshole.

Two, I'm not simply trying to get in her pants. I want to get under her skin, like she's under mine.

But pants . . . pants are a good start.

And it's getting tight in mine.

I scratch my jaw. Part my lips. Try to speak. But my throat is dry. "What?" It's all I can manage to say, and it comes out like a scratch.

"Sorry," she says, backpedaling, sounding as contrite as she did the day I found her by the lake. "Did I offend you?"

Please, offend me more. Offend me so much you ask me to take you home right now.

"You're going to have to try a lot harder to offend me." I eye the couch. "Why don't we sit down?"

That way maybe it won't be so obvious how much I like her plan. How much this is like a fevered, dirty dream, one I don't want to wake up from.

She sits, crossing one bare leg over the other, her polka-dot skirt riding higher to reveal more flesh. I nearly groan out loud—I'll be able to get my hands on those legs soon. Run my palms up her thighs. Spread her open. Touch her where she wants it most. Taste her. Dear God, the prospect of kissing her all over is frying my brain.

Maybe it'll happen tonight? If she wants to conduct this sex symposium over the next week, we'd better get started stat.

Yes, the situation south of the border is indeed escalating.

I keep my eyes fixed on her face. "You want to do a little research in the bedroom?"

She nods, clasping her hands in her lap. "Yes, but I promise it'll be easy. Very manageable."

Yeah, having her naked is something I can absolutely manage easily.

"Whatever you have in mind works for me." I take my time, lift my chin, cautious of seeming too keen. "But why do you want to do *research*?"

"Good question. The answer is that I've only ever had three serious boyfriends, and to be completely frank, none of them were terribly adventuresome."

"That's not going to be a problem with me," I say quickly. Maybe too quickly. But holy fuck. This is like a pot of gold falling into my fucking lap. Maybe I have a leprechaun looking over me.

True, I planned to ask her on a date. To give us a go. But I can work with this brand-new twist. It's a different route, but I bet this path can take us to the same destination.

And hell, will it ever make the drive so much fucking fun.

She breathes deeply, like she's been waiting for a long time to exhale. "Good. I'm glad you don't mind a little light practice."

Light? I was thinking more like hot and heavy, but if that's the term Arden wants to use, who am I to quibble? "I don't mind at all. Not one bit."

She smiles and leans back against the cushions. "God, I was so nervous." She runs her hand through her pretty hair, and I follow her every move, thinking I'll be getting my hands on that hair. She did mention hair-pulling, after all. Fortunately, that's one of my favorite things to do. And Arden's hair, all those lush blonde locks, is prime for yanking, tugging, and wrapping around my fist.

"You don't have to be nervous. I'm glad you asked me. Better me than anyone else."

She drops her hand to my leg, squeezing my

thigh, sending a bolt of lust to every corner of my body. "Please. As if I would go to some other guy."

"Damn straight. I'm your man." I tap my chest. "Now, let's go back to that list. If memory serves, you want to know if you like being taken over the back of the couch, screwing in a pickup truck, making out in an elevator, and having your hair pulled so hard you see stars. Did I get that right?"

Just saying all that out loud sets my skin on fire. Is it my lucky day or what?

Twin spots of pink spread wider across her pretty cheeks as she nods. "I'd say you have that down pat. I thought we could probably tackle everything in a week, and maybe a little taste of each one would give me a better idea."

"Tasting is always a good idea," I say, and my voice goes a little raspier, a little huskier.

Obviously.

Because hell. The prospect of getting my lips all over her is making my mouth water. I could spend all night tasting her everywhere. Exploring her body with my mouth. Yes, this is definitely my lucky day.

"I wrote a list, so there are more items, but that's the general idea. To sample each one."

Damn, do I ever want to see that list. Reading it will be like finding buried treasure, opening a chest full of glittering rubies, sapphires, and diamonds. Her pleasure will be a thousand priceless gems.

"Like when you get a taste at an ice cream

parlor," I say. And a taste leads to a cone. Or a sundae. *With a cherry on top, pretty please.*

"Yes, that's exactly what I'm thinking." She holds up her thumb and forefinger to show a sliver. "Just a little taste is all I need for my research project."

"And when would you like this research to start? Since you have some kind of time limit, I'm assuming ASAP?"

Please say now, please say right fucking now.

She smiles a little impishly, like she's up to something naughty, and, hell, is she ever. She has some very naughty secrets up her sleeve. "Tonight?"

There is a God.

There is a very good God.

"That's one of my favorite words." I clear my throat, grabbing hold of the tiny bit of logic still circling in my brain. "I assume we should establish some ground rules."

She nods vigorously. "Oh, definitely. Like I've said, we can pretty much devote a week to it. Anything longer becomes messy, but I honestly think we can accomplish everything in that time. And beyond that, when the seven days end, I think we also agree to stay friends."

"I can't imagine us not being friends." It's true, but I'm wondering about other ground rules, like her place or mine, and do we need safe words, but sure —the maintenance of the friendship is key too.

"Whew. Me too. That's the most important thing to me. I want you in my life, Gabe."

"I want you in mine." That feels like the truest thing I've voiced all night, and it's freeing, so damn freeing, to admit it, even if it's in this veiled context.

"And another would be if at any point something I ask you to try bothers you—"

I laugh harshly. That might be the most ridiculous thing she's ever said. *Anyone's* ever said. "You don't have to worry about that."

"But I do. I want you to be comfortable, especially because I might ask a lot of questions." Her voice rises at the end, like she wants permission to quiz me.

"Bring it on. I love a dirty talker."

She laughs, glancing down as if she's embarrassed. 'Well, I wasn't thinking like that, exactly."

"Don't worry. We'll get you there in the dirty talk department."

"And I think, too, you can look at this as a practical class. And I suppose you're the teacher."

I hum happily. "Hands-on classes were always my favorite."

She quirks a brow in a question, then shakes her head. "Yes, I suppose it is hands-on."

How else would we be practicing if not hands-on? But I don't say that. If she needs to ease into this, it's fine by me. "And where do you want to start? You want to get out of here and go to my house or to yours?"

She furrows her brow. "Do we need to do that?"

I blink, trying to process what she's saying, and

then it hits me. Duh. I missed the obvious signs. She's trying to break out of her shell. She doesn't want to practice sex at home. She wants to try it in an elevator, or my truck, or maybe even right here.

I glance around, a dirty grin tugging at my lips. "We can start right here if you'd like."

"We can?" Her voice is feathery.

"If that works for you."

She draws a quick breath, then another, like she's gulping for air. "Okay. Let's do it."

Music to my ears.

Since all good sex practice starts with a kiss, I close my eyes and dip my face closer to hers, inhaling her sweet smell, savoring the closeness of her skin. I inch nearer, ready to kiss her breathless. I didn't expect we'd move so quickly, but I have no objections to this pace. None at all, as her honey-scented lotion floats into my nostrils, blurring my mind with the possibilities of pleasure.

But my lips meet nothing but a whoosh of air. My eyes fly open. She's standing above me. I blink, trying to sort out why she leaped up so quickly.

It doesn't look like she jumped away from me. It looks like maybe she missed I was going in for a kiss.

She smooths her hands over her skirt, spins around, and parks her hands on the arm of the couch, bending into an L. "Should we start with spanking?"

"You don't want to ease into it a little more?"

"Go big or go home, right?"

I didn't think lesson one would be ass-smacking, but I'm a flexible guy. Plus, she has a fantastic rear, so I can handle this curveball. I move behind her and bring my hand to her hip to adjust her position.

"We can just do all of this with clothes on, right?"

I stop, the record scratching to a halt. "We can?"

"I meant to say that. Didn't I say that? I had so many things I wanted to say." Her brow pinches as if she's trying to remember. "That's what I said, right?"

"I feel like I'd have remembered that," I say flatly.

"Oh." Her face is crestfallen. "That's what I meant with the sample part. The 'just a taste' part."

My shoulders sag. My libido has been kicked in the nuts. "That's what you meant?"

She stands up straight, smiling like she's proud of herself. "I think the best part of this is we don't have to get naked. All I want is to test out some options here and there. A little biting, a little spanking, and we don't even have to take off our clothes for that. Since we're friends, we can basically act, and that way we won't technically cross any lines."

Kill. Me. Now.

I'm playing Fifty Shades of Blue Balls.

And I'm already halfway there.

15

GABE

I like to think I've seen nearly everything.

I've pulled mangled bodies out of cars that have crashed on the highway. I've witnessed hearts restarting in the back of ambulances as sirens blared. I've been called to some wild scenes at homes, featuring apples and broomsticks that have been stuck in openings where neither fruit nor cleaning supplies belong.

But this?

My best friend asking me to play sex charades?

This is the very definition of being thrown for one hell of a loop the loop. Here I was, sliding into the evening with one thing in mind: finding the best opening to let the woman know how I feel.

And while I was strutting down Feelings Street, she's swept in front of me, cut me off, and taken a sharp left down Let's Act It Out Lane.

I clear my throat. Drag my hand through my

hair. Try to sort out my thoughts. "So we're basically doing wrestling moves?"

"Exactly!" She nods enthusiastically, her smile spreading. Clearly, this project is important to her and delights her. I ought to find a way to share that excitement. But it's admittedly a little hard.

Oh, wait. It's my dick that's still hard. Overeager fucker needs to back off. "Kind of like dance moves? Like we're going to a dance class?"

"Yes. Like we're rehearsing scenes. Think about us as actors on stage. They're not really fencing, but they're going through the motions. Like stage fighting."

"Or stage fucking?"

"Yes, not *real* fucking."

I deflate. Fully this time. This is my unlucky day.

"Because that would be weird. How weird would it be if I asked you to do that?" She laughs, amused, it seems, at the sheer incredulity of someone ever suggesting that. More like sheer fucking awesomeness.

"Ha. So weird. I mean, right? Who does that?" I echo, like I can't believe anyone would ever do that.

"Exactly." Her face seems to light up with relief. "You hear about that happening. A friend asks her friend to help her learn the ropes, but it never works out if you *actually* go through with it. How could it? How could you practice with somebody and not develop feelings for them?"

I part my lips to speak but clamp them shut.

Because I already have feelings for her. They're developed. Past tense. So I answer by way of a shrug.

"Plus, what would happen to our friendship? And, of course, you want to be free to date," she says, as if she's offering me my greatest dreams on a platter—more dating with women who *aren't* her.

I'd like to issue a correction: I want to be free to date *you*. Except Arden's not even thinking along those lines, so I'm going to need to regroup and devise a different strategy to get her to see me that way. But one fact needs to be stated loud and clear. "I don't need to date right now."

She takes a step back, surprise in her features. "You don't?"

I shake my head. "I'm not interested in dating. Also, I can manage a week without it, thank you very much."

"You sure?"

"Well, it'll be hard. But I can manage."

"But I still think it would be unfair of me to limit you. Besides, we're basically going to walk through some naughty scenarios, like a few tutorials. You can guide me, and then I'll have the knowledge I need to make better choices."

She sounds like she's talking about teen pregnancy. Better choices. Knowledge. "You make it sound like a PSA. 'The more you know . . .'"

She laughs. "That's because I'm totally inexperienced in this area. As an example, I've never made love outside."

My jaw drops. "You've never ordered the sex alfresco?"

She raises a hand like she's taking an oath. "Never have I ever."

I affect a big frown. "You're making me so sad right now."

"You'll take pity on me and help me test some new things?" She bats her eyes.

I drape an arm around her and tug her close, sliding into my best playful and friendly voice. "I will definitely take pity on you, my friend. But you do know you can't practice having sex outside with clothes on, right?"

Laughing, she rises on tiptoe and plants a chaste kiss on my cheek, which I like far too much. "I know that. But we can test other things. And by simply testing, rather than actually practicing, we won't ruin our friendship."

Yep. This is going to be a tougher road than I thought. I need to buy some time to figure out how the hell to manage this new twist. "Let's start with talking instead of spanking. How does that sound?"

"I guess spanking wasn't the best way to start?" She fiddles with her watch, which makes me think she's nervous about the whole thing. And I'm not interested in making her nervous. I don't want her to feel awkward. The fact is, it takes some serious ovaries to ask for help in the boudoir. Now that I know what kind of lesson she's after, I don't think that launching right in is the best technique, after all.

"Spanking is a world-class favorite activity, and I guarantee you're going to love it. But let's start by getting out of here so we can discuss your ideas."

There. That'll help me to course correct.

She points to her purse. "Like the list I made?"

"I would very much like to see it."

"Good. There's a lot on it, and it'll help if I bounce ideas off a man. I've discussed plenty of these things with Perri and Vanessa, but I want to get a guy's opinion."

"I'm your guy."

She steps closer, squeezes my shoulder, and whispers sweetly, "Yes, you are."

I'm her guy.

The guy she turned to.

I might not be the guy she wants for more.

Yet.

But the fact that she came to me for help tells me something important—she trusts me. That's a start. A very important start, and one I can build on.

But first, I'm dying to know what the hell is on this naughty list.

16
GABE

Lucky Falls is true to its name.

At least the falls part. The town is edged by a cluster of springs that cascade their way into a gentle river, the kind that sashays and slinks through the town, winding its way under bridges and past shops and markets.

After we say goodbye to our friends, Arden slides into the front seat of my truck, and we shift seamlessly to small talk about Vanessa's event, as if we both know instinctively that this topic's easier for the brief drive. When we reach the river, we park and walk down to the water's edge, finding a smooth boulder. We sit.

Arden kicks off her sandals, her toes dipping into the cool, clear water that gurgles downstream.

The glow of the moon illuminates her face. I do my best to mask my disappointment. Because in a parallel universe I could see us sitting here on this rock and talking about other possibilities, about first kisses, where they might lead to.

Time for the main course of conversation. "All right. Let's dive into this."

She fishes into her bag for the sheet of paper, spreads it open, and goes into all-business mode. "I researched some books. Wrote down the items that most intrigued me. Here is my list. Do you want me to read it to you?"

Let's torture myself some more. "Have at it."

She clears her throat. "Nibbling and biting. We start with little nips and they'd probably lead to bites. Is that how the biting progression works?"

My body hums at the prospect. What I wouldn't give to drag my teeth along that sweet flesh of her neck. To bite into her like a piece of ripe fruit, and savor the taste . . . "I believe that's a fair description."

"And it's fun? Do you think it's fun?"

"Is pizza the greatest food ever invented? Is beer proof of the evidence of God? Is Tom Cruise shorter than me?"

She cracks up. "I feel like that last one doesn't quite belong."

"Honey, he's so much shorter than me. I went from yes, to hell yes, to hell-to-the-mother-fucking yes." I figure the only way to survive the absolute torture of being her at-an-arm's-length sex tutor is to keep it light and make jokes.

"Fine. I'll just add three check marks next to

biting, then." Snagging a pen from her purse, she marks the item off on her list. "Definitely a keeper." She peers at the next option. "Spanking. We've already talked about that."

"And I'm looking forward to swatting your ass." I rub my hands together, then mime swatting.

"My, my. Aren't you eager?"

I point a thumb at my chest. "Big fan of spanking."

"You are?" Her tone is drenched with curiosity.

"Hell, yeah. If it's done right, it should feel good for you too."

"I hope so," she whispers, then ever so briefly she nibbles on one side of her lip, telling me that even though she's never been spanked, she's probably going to like it a hell of a lot.

"What do you think about role-playing?" Her eyes are wide and eager as she tosses out the question.

I think I'm already in love with her list. I'd like to give thanks to the heavens above that she's a woman of books and learning, that she researched thoroughly and penned this most magnificent agenda. "What sort of role-playing do you have in mind?"

She taps her chin. "I could pretend that my kitty cat is stuck in a tree and you could play fireman coming over to rescue my—"

"Pussy?"

A sheet of mortification slides over her face. "Gabe."

"Pussycat?"

"Gabe!"

"Fine, fine. *Fluffy*. I'll rescue your Fluffy."

She swats me. "That's not much better."

"Your furball?"

She balls her hands and pretend punches me.

I grab her fists and meet her gaze. "I think we need to add dirty talking to your list."

"Do we?" Her voice is a little breathy.

"You need to be able to say *pussy*, *cock*, and *dick*. Can we get you there without you turning red?" Lightly, I run a finger down her cheek. Touching her feels a little illicit, but I figure I'm allowed some leeway, as this can't be construed as kissing her.

Clearly.

And sadly.

She turns away, lifts her chin, and whispers, "Pussy."

"Well done."

She squares her shoulders, preparing for a challenge. "Cock."

Mine rises to attention. "Look at that. You're a natural."

She turns to meet my eyes, hers a little fiery. "Dick."

I whistle my approval. "You're a master student at dirty words. All you have to do is say 'Fuck me hard,' and you're going to pass this brief lesson with flying colors."

She parts her lips, then shakes her head, perhaps a little embarrassed now. "I'll save that one for another time."

That saddens me, but all things considered, it'll probably save me from hitting inappropriate levels of steel on the erection-o-meter. "Fuck me hard" is pretty much an iron-clad guarantee I'll go off the arousal charts. I return to her list. "What sort of role-playing interests you?"

"I have this scene in mind . . ."

Scene. My ears like the sound of that. "Set the scene."

"I was seeing myself as a naughty housewife wearing an apron. Can you picture that? When her man comes home and she opens the door wearing only an apron?"

I don't stifle a groan this time. Instead, I let a rumble work its way up my chest and escape my mouth. "Aprons are hot as fuck, especially when there's nothing under them."

"So you want me to open the door wearing heels and an apron with nothing underneath?"

Now.

Right now.

Tomorrow.

Every second.

Because that image will be enough to feed an entire album of fantasies, and it can't happen soon enough. "If that's your fantasy, Arden, I would be happy to knock on the door. You think you'd like that?"

A flicker of desire crosses her eyes. "I think so. That's what I want to find out."

"Are you trying to figure out what men want, or are you trying to learn what drives you wild?"

She licks her lips, stares down at the river. "Both," she whispers, her voice a little bare, a little nervous.

She lowers her head and adds *Aprons* to her list. She glances up at me almost shyly, and all I can think about is her opening the door in an apron that barely covers her breasts, one that exposes the curves of her ass.

I peek at her list, so I don't linger too long on the album of sexy apron images my brain has assembled for me like a playlist.

And the next item isn't any easier to handle.

Striptease.

I shovel a hand through my hair, gritting my teeth.

This is going to be the toughest game of charades I've ever played. "How are you going to do that without removing any clothes?" I rasp out, and my voice practically catches on the grit in my throat.

"Oh, don't worry. This one is easy, actually, because we don't have to touch. I thought maybe I could practice stripping down to a bra and panties." She lowers her voice to a confessional whisper as my internal temperature rivals the surface of Mercury. "I've always wanted to do that. I've never had the chance."

I groan. "What kind of asshats have you been dating? Wait. Don't answer that. I don't want to hear about them. I want to hear about you."

"You do?"

I cup her chin. "Listen to me. You need to be with someone who embraces all that you are. If you want to strip, you need to be with a man you can say that to. If you have no interest in doing a striptease, you need to feel free to say that as well. You need to be you in and out of the bedroom."

"I just want to figure out who that me is in the bedroom."

I want to thank her for letting me help. Because, nudity or not, this is a fucking gift.

She twirls a strand of her blonde hair and inhales. "Would it make you uncomfortable if I stripped to my bra and panties?"

No, that would make me rock fucking hard.

I tap my chin as if seriously considering it. "No. I don't believe that would make me uncomfortable at all," I somehow say with a straight face—and a straight dick too. Pointing straight up at the fucking sky.

"Good." She checks that item on her list then chuckles.

"What's so funny?"

"I was just remembering this time a customer

asked me for a recommendation for a wine to go with the new Reese Witherspoon book club pick. Then she asked me what drink went with JoJo Moyes. Finally, she said, all offhand and casual, 'And what do you think goes with a striptease?'"

I laugh. "Very clever. She was trying to hide her true request. And what did you tell her?"

She raises a brow, her eyes twinkling. "A sparkling white, of course."

The way she says it, a little flirty, a little playful, tells me Arden is definitely game for stripping and, it seems, game for this whole damn experience.

"What else is on that little treasure map?" I peer at the list and spot the next item. "Whoa. Sex in an elevator?"

I definitely don't want to mime that.

"Sorry, that's misleading. I wrote that down as something to do in the future. It could be kissing in an elevator. But look, you don't actually have to give me a kiss. That's totally unfair to ask. We can do that thing where maybe you push me against the wall, grab my wrists, and lift them over my head?" Her voice is a little husky, a little smoky, and that sound tells me she likes the idea more than a little.

That's why "treasure map" is precisely right—this is the path to all her secret desires. Even if we're not acting them out all the way, maybe this list will guide me to winning her all the way over.

I tap the paper. "If we do that *thing* where I push you against the wall, grab your wrists, and lift them above your head, you really should be kissed into blissful oblivion."

I let my gaze linger on her, cataloging her reaction, the way a little murmur seems to escape her lips and how her eyes dance. "Blissful oblivion sounds nice."

I swipe a strand of hair off her neck. "You should feel blissful oblivion."

"I should?"

"Do you know what it feels like? To have sex so good you get lost in it?" My body vibrates with lust, and I clench my fists to remind myself not to touch her.

"I'm not sure."

"I bet you'd look stunning in that state."

Her lips part the slightest bit, like an invitation. "Would I?"

Our gazes lock. "You would."

She casts her eyes down, kicks her toes in the water, and gazes downstream, perhaps clearing her thoughts too.

Needing to cool down, I cut the tension. "If I'm understanding this correctly, you're enlisting me to do sex charades for a week?"

Her laughter fills the night air. "Sure, we'll be mimes."

"Sex mimes." I shake my head in disbelief. "I just signed up to be a sex mime for seven days. Next thing I know, you're going to tell me you require dry-humping services."

Her eyes widen, flickering with excitement that's dangerously attractive. "Is that something you want to do?"

Yes and no and yes. I don't want to dry hump her. I want to fuck her for real. I want to tear her clothes off and get inside her. But dry humping isn't child's play. It can be crazy hot if it's done right.

"It's not my list, honey." I scan the paper, pointing at *Talk openly about sex*. "I'd say we're pretty much already checking off that one."

She smiles. "It seems we are. Gold star?"

"Gold star and an A-plus." I check out the final items, stopping at one in particular. "That's bold."

Mutual masturbation.

She answers at the speed of light. "Again, that's one for me for later. This is only a wish list."

Yeah, all my wishes.

I nudge her with my elbow, raise an eyebrow salaciously. "I would say that's the very definition of a wish list."

She laughs nervously, her pen slicing across the page, crossing it out. "I should cross that off."

I wrap my hand around the pen and ask gently, "Have you ever?"

She shakes her head.

"Do you want to?"

She looks up at me. "Do I?"

"Do you?"

"Is it hot?"

"So fucking hot."

Her voice is breathy. "It sounds hot."

"Let me know if you change your mind."

"I will."

It requires a moment, maybe several, but I tear my gaze away from her, returning to the list. "Hmm. We're missing something."

"We are?"

"There's an item that ought to be on here." I tell her what it is.

She beams as if I've just revealed that I planted a tree that grows money and diamonds in her backyard. "Yes, that's a great idea."

She grabs her pen and adds it to the list. "In fact, do you want to do that tomorrow?"

"It's a date."

And in some ways, I suppose it is. And perhaps I've achieved what I set out to do tonight—snag a date with my favorite person. We're taking a detour, but I'm game to see where this unexpected fork in the road leads.

17

ARDEN

It's the crack of dawn.

The sun blasts brightly through the windows, and I trudge to the door to answer the knock, rubbing my eyes, still bleary with sleep.

Perri and Vanessa stand on my porch, freshly scrubbed, with matching ponytails. *Morning witches*.

Perri parks her hands on her hips and stares down her nose at me. "Hello? Did you forget it's Morning Pilates day?"

I groan. "Otherwise known as International Torture Day. Tell me again why Pilates exists?"

Vanessa stands next to her, head cocked, wagging her finger at me. She pokes my belly. "If you think Pilates is torture, you should try a Zumba class."

I shudder. "Even the name is terrifying,"

"Pilates is good for you. It helps me chase down bad guys in a single bound," Perri says.

I shake my head. "Grapefruit is good for you too, but I'm not scarfing down that citrus at six a.m. on a Sunday."

Vanessa points at me. "That's the irony of your grumbly face. You don't hate exercise. You just hate mornings."

"Call me Garfield," I grumble. "Seriously, why do you insist on morning exercise? And if you do, why aren't we taking a class in sleep? I heard there's a gym that offers a class in napping."

Perri stares at me with saucer-wide eyes. "Please tell me that's not a thing."

Vanessa chimes in. "I've heard that too. It's like a class for new parents who are really tired and don't have a chance to nap. They go to a gym and get sleep masks and cozy beds, and they nap in a class."

Perri scoffs. "That is the height of a first-world offering. It's like taking a class in cuddling. Or hugging."

Vanessa shakes her head. "Disagree. Have you ever hugged someone who didn't know how to hug? It can be very unpleasant. Vise-like, clammy, or flaccid hugs should be outlawed."

"No, the word 'flaccid' should be outlawed," I offer, gesturing for them to come inside.

"You hate the word 'flaccid'?" Perri asks as I shut the door behind them.

"I hate the idea of *flaccid*. So the word might as well go away too. Am I right or am I right?"

"Darling, don't we all want to eliminate flaccidness from the world," Vanessa says, and I offer a palm to high-five.

Vanessa smacks back, and so does Perri. Then my redhead friend grabs my arms, spins me around, and points me upstairs. "Go get your sexy little yoga pants on, Garfield. It's Pilates or bust, and no nap for you."

Harrumphing loudly for effect, I head upstairs, splash some cold water on my face, then yank my hair back in a tight ponytail. I stare at my reflection, and a devilish little smirk appears on my face as I recall last night. It was crazy, maybe even daring to ask Gabe for guidance. Yet it worked. It truly seemed helpful to chat with him.

I already feel more informed and a little more empowered. I'm excited about seeing him today for our mission.

So excited it gives me a huge blast of energy—something I didn't expect to feel at the torturous hour of six in the morning. I make a quick change into workout clothes and return downstairs with a peppy smile. "Okay, let's go, girls."

"Whoa. Did you have a personality transplant with a happy puppy upstairs?"

"Can't a girl be full of energy in the morning?" I ask as we leave my house and walk to the Pilates studio in the middle of town.

"Not you. You look like you have a dirty little secret. Did you have a man hidden away in your bathroom who gave you a quickie while we waited down below?"

"Please." I glance around, then lower my voice to a whisper. "But I did decide to take the bull by the horns."

Vanessa mimes riding a bull. "Tell me more, cowgirl."

"Yes, that exactly. Reverse cowgirl. Well, sort of. I'm going to experiment a little. Learn some more about what I might like." I don't keep secrets from Perri and Vanessa, dirty or otherwise. These ladies are like sisters. I'm an only child, but we grew up together, and I've known them my whole life. My best friends are my family.

"I've decided I'm done with being too vanilla. I asked Gabe to help me."

Vanessa stops in her tracks, slamming an arm against my chest. "Oh no, you didn't? Like you're going to do a *let's get it on* tutorial?"

"Please, no. This won't be hands-on. More like mouths-on." But that's not the best analogy either. I backpedal. "I mean, we're going to talk through some stuff. Go over a bunch of different options. Discuss what I might like and how to ask for it. It's going to work out so perfectly. It's like a dress rehearsal before a big show."

Perri clears her throat loudly. Deliberately. "You do know that a dress rehearsal means you go on stage and put on your costumes and go through all the motions?"

"I do know that." I smack her butt. "See? Isn't it better that I practice with him rather than you?"

She jumps away and gives me the side-eye. "Yeah, I don't want you to spank me, sweetie. Unless you're six two, inked, and built like a Greek god."

"And if you find that man, please share him," Vanessa adds, but I flash back to last night and wonder if it's a Greek god she wants or someone else—namely Perri's brother.

"How exactly does your sex school start?"

"Last night we talked through things on my list, so that was essentially the first lesson."

"What's the next lesson?" Perri asks.

I tell them what Gabe and I have planned for this afternoon.

"We've done that with you before," Vanessa points out.

"I know, but it will be interesting to go with a man and get the guy's perspective."

"I bet perspective's not the only thing Gabe wants to give you," Vanessa says in a low voice.

But she's wrong. I'm not his type. That's why I chose perfectly. This will be one week of learning, with no risk of crossing into the romance zone. We can safely stay friends and focus on my new sex-education syllabus.

And I'm as ready as I'll ever be for lesson number two.

18

GABE

It seemed like a good idea at the time.

But now?

Now I think I'm going to require a longer-than-usual run if I expect to survive sex toy shopping with Arden.

I hate shopping.

Wait, hate is too strong a word.

I don't detest anything.

Except for drunk drivers, arsonists, and the designated hitter rule.

Also, littering and broccoli.

But those are all reasonable hates.

Shopping is more like something I strive to avoid the same way I aim to dodge day-old bagels, warm beer, and community pools.

But when you're shopping for sex toys with a woman you want to screw, well, that requires a whole new approach.

That's why I run this morning alongside my cousin. I meet up with Tom, who recently moved to the neighboring town with his new woman, Finley. Tom's a brainiac and a roller-coaster designer, so I ask him to tell me about his new projects.

Listening to him talk about engineering feats of daring keeps me in the right zone.

The no-thinking-about-sex zone.

The conversation is solely on work, and it helps. After a few miles, he's done. "I'll catch you next time," he says. "And I promise I'll regale you with exciting details on how to make a ride go upside down."

I give him a quick tip of the cap. "The regaling is on the calendar."

I continue without him, because my mission requires *extra*.

Extra running.

Extra focus.

A lot of extra miles to get out of the sex-centric zone I've been living in. It's a proven medical fact that men require at least a half dozen miles of hard running or several hours on the StairMaster before the constant thought of sex vacates the brain for even a few minutes.

Over the river and through the woods I go, putting distance between the swirl of dirty thoughts and my stark reality. I pass seven miles, then hit eight, adding a long workout at the gym with weights. As I lower the barbell on my final set, I've slipped into a blissful, blank mind-set.

There's one more thing I need to seal the deal and live in this state a little longer.

Seeing my parents.

There is no bigger sex buzzkill than a visit with Mom and Dad, so I pop by for a little breakfast. My mom whips up some spectacular scrambled eggs with provolone cheese and mushrooms, and my father's coffee ought to be worshipped by baristas the world over.

As I chew, Mom chats about how my sister, Kim, is doing with her third pregnancy, how big her belly is, and how awful she's feeling trying to move.

Yup.

All the details of Kim waddling around are adding up to a blank sex slate upstairs, and I couldn't be happier.

By the time I return home, tired from the run, stuffed from breakfast, and filled with images of my basketball-belly sister, I can't escape the no-sex zone.

This is not an easy state for a man to achieve. We can only successfully reach this sexual tabula rasa, say, 1 percent of the day.

Wait. That's far too generous.

More like 0.2 percent.

But when you're there, you feel like you can master string theory and write a symphony.

I hum a few notes from Beethoven's "Ode to Joy," since that's about the only classical music I know, and damn, that shit is good. Beethoven could write some badass melodies.

Since I'm all about expanding my mind for the precious few minutes that it's uncluttered by sex thoughts, I decide I ought to try to learn quantum physics. I down a huge glass of water, grab my phone, and find a podcast on the topic. I sync my phone to my speaker and head into the bathroom, strip out of my clothes, and turn on the hot water.

I close the shower door, stepping under the stream, zoning in on the podcaster as he talks of atoms and electrons. I run the soap over my body, letting my brain be a sponge soaking up all this new information.

". . . added wave crests result in brighter light," the voice says, and my mind hiccups on that word—*crest*.

It reminds me of something else. Something a woman's pleasure might do.

Stop.

Stay focused.

I square my shoulders and train my ears on the podcast host as I run shampoo through my hair.

". . . objects exist in a haze of probability."

Haze.

Like how Arden would look in a sex-drenched—

No. Don't go there.

As he drones on about the size and speed of moving objects, I'm not sure I can hold onto this rarefied state. I'm slipping, falling, flailing back to the 99 percent land.

All these words make me think of her.

Of toys.

Of shopping.

Of orgasms cresting. Of the hazy look in her eyes. And her list. Dear God, her fucking list. All the things on that list I don't want to mime.

I want to *do*.

As I run the soap over my body, my hand strays down my stomach, lower still, and I take my dick in my palm.

I give in to the material world of pleasure and sex, back where I, evidently, belong.

Gripping my shaft, I run through Arden's wish list, item by item, as if I'm considering every dish at a rich and scrumptious buffet. My fist shuttles up and down my cock, the soap slicking its path.

She wants me to ring the doorbell so she can answer it in an apron and nothing else.

I suck in a harsh breath imagining where that moment might lead. Undoing the strap, exposing her tits, letting the fabric fall to the floor.

A shudder slams into my body, and my cock hardens even more, doing a most excellent impression of an iron spike. My fist grips it tighter, racing up and down my length.

My mind becomes a flip book of images. Her practicing a striptease. Pushing me down on the couch, grinding against me, rubbing what I bet is a fantastic ass into my lap.

My balls tighten as I picture how good that ass would feel.

Then I switch the scene to her bedroom. She's stripped to nothing but her own raw desire. Lights dimmed. Legs spread. Fingers flying furiously.

What is she picturing?

Pleasure rattles through me, rolls down my spine as I try to imagine what she's getting off to.

I want it to be me.

I want her wild with pleasure, riding the edge.

I want to discover her like that, put her on all fours, slide into her and send her soaring.

I want to make her come so fucking hard. Just like she's doing to me right now. My orgasm barrels through me, rushing under my skin until I shoot.

I breathe out roughly, cursing.

It's not the first time I've pictured her, but it's the first time I've let myself finish to her.

As I rinse off, I learn that if an object is heated sufficiently, it starts to emit light at the red end of the spectrum as it becomes red-hot.

Red-hot. Sounds about right.

Maybe I did learn something after all.

I turn off the podcast and head to meet Arden.

19

ARDEN

I scurry through the bustling shop on a Sunday afternoon, adding a few last-minute additions to the travel shelves and helping a pair of lovely ladies find just the right book on raising an adopted baby.

"This one looks perfect," says the gal with the long braid slinking down her back as she clutches the book to her chest.

"You'll love it. I've sent many soon-to-be adoptive parents home with it," I tell them.

The other woman drapes an arm around her and squeezes, then meets my gaze. "Thanks for your time."

"No problem."

This is why I love what I do. Books aren't simply a door to another world. They truly help people. They are wonderful treasures to guide individuals, couples, and families through new life situations, and they're also the best form of travel I've ever known.

Because I read, I've visited India, I've knelt at the feet of kings, I've battled dragons, and I've learned new words and worlds.

Books led me to the world I'm visiting later today. They've made me curious about the landscape of sex, and the cities on the map of pleasure I've completely missed. I want to embark on uncharted trails, discover a new country, a place where I'm free to explore. Good thing I have a Sherpa.

As the ladies leave the store, I grab my bag and make my way to the door then remember an order that's due tomorrow. "Madeline," I call out. "We're expecting the new coffee-table books tomorrow morning. Did you—?"

She points to the door like a drill sergeant, searing me with her eyes. "It's your day off, boss lady. Go."

"But..."

She shakes her head. "I already checked the tracking order, and it's all set. On its way."

I breathe a big sigh of relief. "Stop being so damn good at your job."

She nods solemnly. "I'll try to steal from the till and rip the pages out of books later. Now go, or I will spread a rumor that you've never read *The Time Traveler's Wife* and you named the cats Henry and Clare simply from the movie."

"Lies. Vicious lies." I make my way to the door, crossing the threshold, then I pop my head back in. "One more thing."

Madeline crosses her arms and shakes her head. "Goodbye, Arden. It's called Sunday."

I heed her advice and step outside, bumping into a woman from the book club—Sara, the patron saint of car blow jobs and spankings.

"Hi, Sara."

Her laugh lines crinkle when she smiles. "Arden, I was hoping to find you. I need to know what kind of wine goes with the new Jandy Nelson book."

"Her writing is sublime, isn't it?"

Sara brings her hands to her chest. "It is absolutely incandescent."

"It's like she has access to another dictionary, to a whole new palette of words and colors. Everything is vibrant, and that means you need a sauvignon blanc when you read Jandy Nelson. That wine is bursting with vibrant, fresh flavors."

Sara's eyes sparkle. "That sounds perfect. I'm going to spend the afternoon getting lost in a good book with a delicious wine. You're a wine and book matchmaker."

I smile and say goodbye as Sara heads into the store. Madeline can handle the rest of Sara's reading needs. After all, both of these ladies know how to speak for themselves. Madeline talked herself into a weekend job in my store and has refused to leave ever since, going from strength to strength to become the right-hand woman I now can't be without, adding more responsibility every month. And Sara? Well, Sara craves giving blow jobs on deserted roads and isn't afraid to ask for it but also enjoys her best life reading award-winning literature, drinking fine vintages, and spending her time with an amazing group of friends.

People are so much more than we see on the surface. David only saw me as a nice, vanilla, bookish girl. But beneath the cover, there's more to me, and I want to know what's written on all my pages.

As I walk down the block, I check out my reflection in the window of a black BMW. A peach tank top, a black lacy skirt, and cute sandals. *Looks like date attire.* I talk sternly back to my reflection. "It's only an outing. You've been on a million of them with Gabe."

Yet it's a little different this time, and different isn't a bad thing, I'm realizing. I like the little bubbles of anticipation that float around inside me. I like the heady feeling under my skin. I enjoy that I'm going to learn something new.

As I turn onto my block, Gabe is pulling up, cutting the engine on his truck. He strides up to me on the sidewalk, that easy grin on his face, the sun glinting off his aviator shades. He takes them off, and I'm speechless for a moment.

Because I know new things about my good friend.

Gabe thinks I should be kissed into blissful oblivion.

So do I.

Gabe likes dirty talk.

I think I might too.

I've been talking dirty in my head for longer than I think I knew. I've been saying naughty words to myself when I'm alone and imagining the kind of man who'd want to explore my body the way I want to be discovered.

Gabe believes a striptease would be mighty hot.

I feel hot, so damn hot.

My skin heats, and a flush crawls up my chest.

I tell myself it's from the summer day.

But that's a lie. Suddenly, I'm thinking about Gabe in a whole new way.

A way I shouldn't allow.

20

ARDEN

Keep it light, keep it friendly.

"Hey there, Coach."

He lifts an eyebrow. "Coach. I like it. Are you ready for a shopping spree, my new sex athlete? Sex-thlete."

"Do I need my platinum card, Coach?"

"Depends how many orgasms you want."

"Hmmm. Preferably multiple." Damn, it *is* fun to talk about sex so freely with a guy.

"That's definitely the best kind." He heads to the passenger door, and I follow. "Let's find a dolphin for your clitorisaurus."

A laugh bursts from my throat. "Did you really just say what I think you said?"

He swivels around, wearing a stoic expression. "It's the scientific term."

"Then I would presume a cock ring would be used on your cock-o-rex?"

I mentally high-five myself for saying *cock* so easily. It's like the word has been set free after saying it out loud last night for one of the first times in my life.

Cock. Cock. Cock. Cock-a-doodle-doo, indeed.

Gabe raises an appreciative brow. "No more blushing when you dirty talk, I see."

"Cock." I smile, showing off my skills.

"Speaking of, mine's not of the cock-o-rex species. That variety has tiny little balls," he says, wiggling his arms like a Tyrannosaurus rex's little limbs.

"Perhaps it would work on your shaftceratops."

Hot damn. I'm getting good.

His lips curve up in a playful grin. "Or maybe we could stick with names from actual dinosaurs. In that case, Giganotosaurus would be the way to go. Because . . . *giant*."

I tsk-tsk him. "Are you forgetting there was a Megalosaurus once upon a time?"

"Dammit. You're right. Mega is bigger. But my Diplodocus isn't the star of the show today," he says, tossing out one more actual dinosaur name. "Let's go shop for you."

He opens the door to his truck, and I slide inside. He joins me, turning the key.

"Hey, Gabe?"

"Yeah?"

"I know we're not even at the sex toy shop, but you made it really easy already with the jokes."

Maybe that's why I can rattle off these words with such ease.

He flashes me a grin. "Humor is my favorite lubricant."

"I'm serious," I say firmly.

"So am I." He pulls away from the curb. "Also, I'm glad you're feeling comfortable."

"Me too." I shoot him a friendly smile, my reassurance that I know the score. "How was your morning?"

"Good. Saw my mom and dad. Went for a run. Learned some quantum physics."

That piques my interest. "Ooh, what did you learn?"

"That some things make other things move fast and hot."

I laugh again. "Sounds like it stuck with you."

"What did you do this morning?" He flicks on the turn signal at the end of my block.

"Perri and Vanessa held me hostage so I could be thoroughly tortured by the Pilates instructor. Those machines are insane."

He shudders. "I don't understand how anybody chooses to exercise on that crazy contraption. It's like a modern-day torture rack. One time, we were called to a Pilates studio because someone was actually injured on the bench."

I thrust my arms in the air. "That is literally all I needed to know. I'm going to share that with

Vanessa and Perri, because I would do anything to get out of that class."

"You need to be careful. Those places are like death traps."

"What actually happened on the call?"

"Did you eat breakfast today?"

"Yes. Why?"

He turns down Main Street. "I can't tell you because I just had the dashboard cleaned."

"You're joking, right?"

"No. Yes. Maybe. Look, I've seen injuries from sex, and I won't tell you to stay away from that type of exercise."

I laugh at his designation of sex as exercise. "Pilates does make you flexible," I add, a little flirty since that's the name of the game today.

"How long have you been doing it?"

"Couple years."

"Forget what I said. It's not dangerous at all. Keep doing it. It'll give you great flexibility in your sex life for years to come." He winks at me.

"You're so thoughtful. Looking out for my sex-leticism down the road."

"Like a good coach."

I raise an eyebrow. "And is running good for your sex life?"

He nods proudly. "Stamina, baby."

And now I wonder how Gabe's is in bed.

Stop. Just stop.

"How many miles did you run?"

"Eight."

Oh God, he must have great stamina.

"That's good cardio," I say, deadpan.

"And I have great stamina."

And I'm getting hot and bothered.

"And I'm flexible," I add, and now this is it—I have to stop flirting. "But running. That's basically a modern form of hell."

"But how else am I going to burn off those coconut bars you're making me?" He swings the truck to the right, and we head down a long stretch of road that'll take us away from Lucky Falls.

"I'm making you coconut bars?"

"You didn't think you were the only one getting something out of this? I'm happy to teach you, but I'm going to require some payment in the form of food."

I laugh, only too happy to provide for him in that department. "How about some coconut bars and dinner sometime this week?"

"It's a deal if it includes the striptease."

Ohhhh. I picture undressing in front of Gabe, and it terrifies me. "Are you serious?"

He lifts an eyebrow. "Are you?"

Am I? I let the scene play out, returning to the image of stripping down to my sexiest La Perla panties and bra, and I no longer feel terror. I feel thrills. Or perhaps I feel both, and I like the cocktail, thank you very much. "Yes. I think I am."

A grin that reaches halfway to Naughty Town

spreads across his face. "You've got yourself a deal. But aside from the torture rack, did you enjoy your time with your girls?"

I love that he calls them that. Vanessa and Perri are most definitely my girls. "I always love seeing them. Is that kind of crazy? I've known them since we were five, but we still have something to talk about every single time."

"It's like that with great friends, isn't it?"

I nod as we cruise past lush green hills rich with grapevines and billboards beckoning travelers to stop for wine tastings and to sample all sorts of grapes. "We're like sisters. We went on a trip when we were younger—we were thirteen, and our parents sent us to visit Vanessa's grandparents on their horse ranch for two weeks during the summer—and the security guard at the airport asked if we were triplets."

Gabe chuckles. "The blonde, the redhead, and the brunette."

"Exactly! And sure, we could be fraternal triplets, but then he said, 'You all look alike,' and I think it's because we had that sister energy. That connection."

"I definitely see that in the three of you."

"We thought that was the best compliment in the world. My mom said to the guy, 'No, but they wish they were.' And that was true. We wanted to be sisters so we could be together all the time. To hang out together, play cards, watch movies, go to the mall, get our ears pierced—we wanted to do everything. And now, as we all race toward thirty, we still love our time as a trio."

"It's a rare and precious gift to stay friends that long. I'm glad you have it. I'm glad they're your family."

"Me too." I smile since he gets it. He completely understands our tight bond. "Speaking of family, how is your pops doing?"

Gabe offers a small smile. "I saw him a few days ago, and he kept talking about a dog he missed. A female schnauzer, he insisted. He only wanted the female schnauzer. But he never had that kind of dog. He always had collies."

"What did you say when he was talking about a dog he didn't have?"

"I kept reminding him of Daisy and Violet. Those were his collies. Eventually, we talked about other things. Baseball, the fire department, and the mac and cheese that Emily—my nana, his wife—used to make him. He had no trouble remembering the recipe for the mac and cheese," Gabe says with a laugh.

"Did he give you the recipe?"

"Yeah, it was basically cheese, more cheese, and even more cheese."

"Sounds yummy."

"It was his favorite thing to serve me when I was at their house as a kid. All things considered, I guess he's doing okay." He drums his fingers on the steering wheel. "You know, he's the reason I kick your ass at Words with Friends."

"He is?" Gabe's talked about his grandfather frequently, and someday I hope to meet the man he admires so much.

Gabe's voice tightens, like this is hard for him. "When he first realized he was struggling with his memory, he pulled me aside and told me he was going to give me the most important piece of advice ever: 'Do crossword puzzles, young man. Exercise your brain. Don't be like me.'"

A lump rises in my throat. I knew Gabe loved his puzzles and his grandpa, but I didn't make the connection before—that it was the older man's words of wisdom that spurred him on. They led him to keep that part of him—his mind—as active and well-oiled as his body. It's far too easy to neglect the brain, but that isn't a choice Gabe has made, and that's hella sexy.

I'm tempted to squeeze his bicep, to run a hand lightly through his hair, something, anything. Instead, I keep my hands to myself and use my words. "You're pretty damn sharp, Harrison, so I'd say both the brain and body workouts are doing the trick."

"Thank you." He gives me a quick glance out of the corner of his eye. "Same to you."

Tingles swoop down my body from the compliment, and we're quiet for a moment as I stare out the window, savoring the delicious view of curving hills and winding roads that bend through the towns I love.

As if he can read my mind, he says, "We live in a beautiful place."

I sigh contentedly. "The only time I've lived elsewhere was college in Berkeley, and though I loved it, I'm so glad I moved back."

"I'm glad my parents retired here when my pops settled here after Nana passed. Gave me an excuse to move away from the city."

"I'm glad you moved here too, even though it's sad that that's the reason."

He tips his forehead to a sign up ahead. "Welcome to Petaluma. Now, why don't they say, 'Welcome to Petaluma, home to a fantastic taqueria, the closest Target, and one helluva sex shop'?"

"You'd think the chamber of commerce would be all over that." I gaze at the sign, but a gray mass on the side of the road snags my attention.

No! There's an animal on the shoulder. I jerk out my hand. "Gabe! Look!"

He slows down then pulls over. We get out and walk around, and I gasp when I see an owl on the edge of the gravel, exactly where an owl shouldn't be. "Is he okay?"

"I'm not sure." Gabe bends to one knee, taking a look at the creature, which is sitting up but not trying to fly away. "I'm no vet, but I'm betting he has an injured wing."

"Should we take him to Wild Care?" I ask, urgency coloring my tone.

"Definitely. But we need to be careful how we move him. You stay next to the little guy."

I do as instructed, kneeling next to the small bird with a spotted brown coat. "You're going to be okay, little buddy," I tell him, though tears prick my voice. I don't know what to do for him, but as I peer back at Gabe, who's grabbing a blanket from the bed of the truck, he seems to know exactly how to help.

He rejoins me on the gravel. Gently, with steady hands, he slides the hurt bird onto the blanket. Gabe is the picture of cool calm. "Go sit in the cab and put your seat belt on. You need to hold this little guy."

My heart speeds even faster. I do as he says, buckling in. A few seconds later, he carefully lifts the bird in the blanket then sets him on my lap. The animal wiggles a bit. "Just keep him here, nice and safe, okay? If he tries to wriggle out, put the blanket over him, since they like darkness."

"I can do that." My voice is as jumpy as my skittering pulse.

Gabe slides back in and starts the engine. The hair on my arms stands on end as I stare at the hedgehog-size creature with frightened yellow eyes. He's settled down a little.

"It's instinct for you, isn't it?" I ask.

He glances over at me as he navigates back on the road. "What do you mean?"

I nod to the owl. "This is why you do what you do. You're naturally good at helping."

"Maybe," he says quietly.

"It's not a maybe, Gabe. You knew exactly what to do with this owl. Did you always want to be a fireman? Well, besides being a pitcher?"

"What kid doesn't?"

"But what made it serious for you?"

His expression turns somber. "My nana had a heart condition. She didn't realize it till one night when I was staying with them when I was younger. My pops called 911, and the firefighters were the first ones there. I still remember how unruffled and helpful they were."

"Were you scared?"

"I honestly wasn't, because of those guys. I watched them closely, and paid attention to what they did. They were calm and reassuring, and any time she had any trouble, that's exactly how I tried to be with her — calm and reassuring."

My throat tightens. "Like how you were with Hedwig," I say, glancing at the owl. "Even though Hedwig is a girl in Harry Potter, and I think this owl is a boy. But I'm honestly not sure, since I'm not an owl vet either."

"Arden," he chides, "we are not keeping him."

"I know. But he needed a name." I clear the emotions from my voice as best I can. "Did you know you'd be good at it?"

"I think so, but I also think it felt natural. Like

something I could do. Well, if baseball didn't work out. And that's precisely what happened."

"Do you ever regret that baseball didn't work out?"

"Nah. How many guys get to have the two careers they want? I'm lucky—I got to play ball, and now I can do this. I can help people." He squeezes my leg with his free hand. It's not sexual. It's friendly and comforting, like maybe he knows I'm a little nervous, a little jumpy in the role of his owl paramedic assistant. "And today we're going to help this little guy."

A few minutes later, we take Hedwig into Wild Care and Gabe hands off the owl. After that mission, we head over to The Garden of Eden.

As we walk inside, nerves flutter inside me once more, but I've found talking helps eradicate them. "There's no one I'd rather go sex toy shopping with than the guy who rescued Hedwig the owl."

And it's strange but completely true.

21

ARDEN

There are no windows. The brick exterior boasts a sign for adult pleasures. Inside, the shelves are teeming with battery-operated boyfriends, replicas of penises, vibrating rings, jellies, lubes, and every flavor of edible massage oil under the sun.

There's something for everyone here, including an aisle with a buzzing corn-on-the-cob vibrator, half a woman's torso made of silicone, and . . . feet. Feet of all sizes and colors.

Gabe brandishes a pale plastic one. He mimes running the fake foot in front of his crotch. A blush creeps across my cheeks as he pretends to grind against it, then deepens as he fakes his orgasmic pleasure.

I grab the toy. "Stop. You are not getting it on with a plastic foot."

"I wasn't trying to get it on. I was trying to get off."

I laugh as I set down the toy I'll never buy.

Gabe scans the shelves, and his eyes light up. He points. "We have to go see that." He grabs my hand and guides me to a bright rainbow braid.

I squint, studying the swath of colors. "Should I put that in my hair?"

He laughs, then speaks dryly. "Sure. Or someplace where the sun doesn't shine." He turns it around revealing a silver plug on the other end.

My blush shoots up fifty shades. "And this is why I need help. Because I actually thought—erroneously—that I could buy a rainbow braid for my hair here."

"Look at it this way. You could start a line of butt plug hair extensions."

"Yeah, that's a hard no." But I am curious about something, and since I have a living, breathing man in front of me, one who's pretty damn open, I decide to ask him. I tug his shirt, pulling him closer as I drop my voice. "Would you ever want to use one?"

He straightens. "On myself? No fucking way. Now, if you wanted to use one . . . would it be my first choice? Not necessarily. But if you wanted to try butt stuff, I'd experiment with you."

I don't want to try butt stuff, yet something about his willingness intrigues me. "You would? Even if it's not your thing?"

He shrugs happily. "Of course."

"Why?"

He steps closer. "Because if we were together,

my number one goal would be to make sure you were . . . *satisfied.*" That last word lingers on his tongue, almost like a reassurance. With him, I can't imagine I'd be anything but immensely pleased.

I blink away the thought. I should not be thinking about how good sex with him might be. That's not what this sex-ucation is about. I take a breath, survey the shelves, and spot a curve of raspberry silicone, like a stretched C. I raise a hand. "Okay, maybe this makes me a clueless idiot, but what is that?"

We walk over to what's billed as a couple's vibrator and study it closely. I can't for the life of me figure out where each end of this double-ended device goes, or on whom. "How do you wear this? *Who* wears it?"

Gabe turns it on its side, showing me the instructions on the tag. My mouth parts in an O as I read. "The front of the sex toy hangs on the clitoris, and the rest of it goes inside the woman. Supposedly, it gives great G-spot orgasms *while* engaged in intercourse with a partner. But I don't understand how I'm supposed to have this chunk of plastic in me while I'm having sex."

"Double the pleasure, double the fun?"

"I think it's daunting." But then I remind myself of my mission—to speak up with men. "Do you think it's too daunting?"

He regards the device. "I honestly have no idea, but I'd be game to try it."

That's what I'm learning about Gabe—he's up for anything. That easy way he has seems to extend all the way to the bedroom. He appears to have no hang-ups, just a healthy appetite for experimentation if his partner wants to go into the lab and mix up new formulas for nookie. I'm sure he'd don his white coat and get it on right there beside the test tubes and beakers.

"Would you try it?" His gaze meets mine, and our eyes lock. A rush of sensation spreads down my chest, like fluttering tingles.

"I would try it. I don't know if I'd like it, but I'd try it." My breath comes a little faster.

"What kind of vibrator do you have?"

I smile. "Why do you assume I have one at all?"

He sets his hand on his belly and laughs in an over-the-top fashion. "That's a good one."

"I mean it. How did you know?"

"Are you kidding me?"

"No. I really want to know how you assumed I had one."

He arches a brow. "Arden East, I bet you have more than one."

I smile in a silent admission. I'm liking Naughty Town a lot.

"Exactly." He steps closer. "And to answer how I knew—I knew because you like pleasure. Because you're not getting what you want from your relationships. Because you asked me to help you learn more about men and sex. Ergo, you know how to take care of yourself, but you want to know what to do with all that *desire* when you're with someone."

His eyes sweep up and down my body, making my stomach flip unexpectedly, quickening my pulse. Maybe it's the way he says *desire*. Maybe it's how he looks at me with darkened eyes, or the close quarters we've found ourselves in. Whatever it is, all I want to do is give him the honest truth. My skin is buzzing, and it feels good to talk about sex.

"I have three. A bullet, a lipstick vibrator, and a dolphin."

He swallows, taking his time speaking again. "Lucky dolphin."

I laugh at the obvious joke. "Or maybe I'm the lucky girl."

"Do you carry the lipstick one with you?"

"So I can diddle myself in my car?"

"Or behind the counter at the bookstore?"

"I am most decidedly not taking solo flights at work."

"When do you break them out?"

"At home."

"And which one do you use the most?"

"I like the dolphin best of all. He has most favored nation status." *Holy smokes.* I'm serving it all up. I'm telling him everything. And it feels fantastic. It's freeing. He seems to be enjoying this conversation too, judging from the hint of a smile tugging at his lips.

"Like I said, lucky dolphin," he murmurs as he guides me to the next aisle, and we're in a wonderland of animals: butterflies, dolphins, rabbits. "All right, this isn't your first turn at the menagerie, then. But you did say you wanted to try mutual masturbation."

A rush of heat zips through me, shooting my temperature higher. What is he going to suggest? Does he want us to do that even though I'd instigated a clothes-on rule? Nerves mix with a strange new excitement. "We don't have to," I quickly say, because I can't bear the thought of crossing a line, even as it entices me.

He cuts me off, looking me straight in the eyes. "I know. Believe me, I know. But this is what I'm thinking. You're trying to move beyond your comfort zone. Learn new things, right?"

"Yes."

"Then I want you to do something for me."

I've no idea what he wants me to do, but a delicious heaviness throbs between my legs, and I think I'll like whatever he says. "Okay."

"Tell me what you like about the one you're using."

"Tell you?"

"Yes."

"Right now?"

"Yes."

I look around. A skinny woman in black with

earplugs works the counter, and a redhead in a plaid skirt is hanging up a sexy nurse costume. Nearby, a couple covered in ink checks out strap-ons.

"And how does this help?" I whisper as we regard a shelf of dolphins and rabbits.

"You said you wanted to be able to voice what you like in bed. Do you want to practice by telling me what you like about the dolphin?"

Sparks ripple across my skin at his request, leaving a trail of gooseflesh in their wake. I do want to tell him. I do want to say what I like.

I point to a light-blue dolphin, take a deep breath, and draw on desire—the desire to speak my mind with a man. *I can do this. I can say this.* "I like the dolphin because . . ." I pause. I've never been this vocal before. I picture my solo rides, how I close my eyes, lie back on my bed, and imagine trying new positions, exploring new lands, as I pleasure myself. "Because it goes deep. Because it feels good inside me, and outside."

The blue in his eyes turns fiery. "The dolphin makes you feel like you're being touched by someone who knows how to take care of your needs?"

I shiver, my knees going a little weak. My mind is turned all the way on. "Yes, like my lover is attuned to me."

His voice is raspy. "And knows how to touch you just right. Knows how to make your skin tingle, how to move his hands over you so the world slips away."

A quick breath falls from my lips, as my body becomes electric. "That sounds amazing," I whisper.

His eyes are intense, shining with something that looks dangerously like pure lust. "Because he doesn't take the gift of your body for granted. Because he asks, and you tell him. Now, tell me—so you can practice saying it—what do you picture when you're close?"

The flame in his eyes jumps to me, and I'm ignited as I cycle through my go-tos then whisper, "My mind . . . flips through different images. But sometimes it's words. Things I say, things I picture a lover doing to me."

He inches closer, and the air crackles and hums between us. "Like what you want to say when you're about to come?"

I nod, my temperature soaring from that one word—*come*. I ache everywhere. I ache between my legs with the delicious, torturous need to come. Not now, not here, but soon. "Things I've never said out loud," I whisper, my face hot.

"Dirty, sexy words?"

"Yes."

"What words?"

I glance around. The silence in the store is deafening. The pounding of my blood is intense. When I've gone sex toy shopping with my friends, I felt like a naughty schoolgirl, giggling and making jokes. Now, with a sexy man as my companion, I feel naughty in a whole new way.

A sexier way.

A seductive way.

It's like he's seducing me—unintentionally, I'm sure—with his dirty talk, but when he's this close, uttering those words and smelling so masculine, so damn strong, I nearly groan out loud.

Still, I don't want to go too far in the store. Some things are too private.

"You don't want to say it here?"

I shake my head.

"I get that. I don't want you to move beyond your comfort zone right now. But I have an idea. And it'll help you with your exploration."

"What is it?"

"Let's get you a new rabbit. Something that goes deep, how you like it. Something that makes you feel like you're being fucked by a man who wants you, and a man who knows how to please you."

God, I think I might come from *his* words. That's what I want. That's what I need. I pick up a rabbit with more speeds than I've ever used. "This one."

"I'll buy it, then you report back to me."

I flinch, surprised at his directions. "Do you want me to text you?"

"It'll help you with your dirty talking. Try the rabbit, and then tell me how you felt."

"Let you know what I say when I'm alone?" The fire roars, burning bright inside me.

"Isn't that what you want? To be able to say those things in the heat of the moment?"

Desperately.
"Yes."
"This is the first step."
And I'm going to take it.

22

ARDEN

That night when I'm alone, I'm ready, so ready. I don't even need a dirty book or a Tumblr feed.

I'm aching and swollen between my legs, and when I lie down on my bed and slide my hand inside my panties, I'm slick. From spending the whole damn day with Gabe. I turn on the vibrator, and I know it won't take long at all.

Pleasure spirals in me, and I moan, and I fantasize. I imagine I'm saying all sorts of things to a lover.

A few minutes later, I'm coming, and it feels glorious.

But I want more. I want so much more . . .

Out of nowhere, or perhaps out of today, Gabe's face flickers before me, his lips, his smile.

For a moment, I try to resist. But my body is beyond fighting.

With those images, I go again, warring with my brain.

I try to shove away thoughts of him.

He's a friend, only a friend.

But I'm seeing him take off his shirt, revealing his chest, then dipping his thumbs in the waistband of his shorts and shucking them off.

Holy fuck.

I just undressed my best friend for the first time, and God, he looks beautiful naked.

He looks even better when he climbs on the bed and buries his face between my legs, devouring me. I pretend he's here, and I'm telling him exactly what I want.

I come harder and longer.

When I turn off the rabbit, waves of pleasure still radiate through my legs like electric pulses. They crest over me, a true high, as I grab my phone and text him.

Arden: Hi . . . I did homework.

Gabe: I can't wait for your book report.

My thumbs hover over the keys. Am I doing this? Am I going to tell him what comes out of my mouth?

I think of the book club ladies and their boldness. Of Madeline and her confidence on the job.

This is what it means to be a woman today—to own your choices.

I'm confident with my friends.

I'm good at my job.

And I want a rich and layered sex life.

Here goes.

23

ARDEN

I send a naughty text.

Arden: The rabbit worked . . . I used it twice.

Gabe: Excellent . . . glad to hear my hopping friend made you happy.

Arden: I was loud.

Gabe: Loud is so very good.

Arden: I said all sorts of things . . .

Gabe: Want to tell me?

God, I do. More than I thought I would. But if I'm going to woman up, I need to woman all the way up. I slide my finger over his contact info and hit his name.

He answers immediately. "Does this mean I get an oral report?"

He makes me laugh. He always makes me laugh. And maybe his laughter is the lubricant I need. "I want to practice. To say out loud to you all the things I think when I get off."

"Say them to me." His voice is husky, commanding.

I close my eyes, hearing the echo of my own words. "Fuck me."

He murmurs, "That's a great one."

"Spread my legs. Oh God, spread them wider." My breath stutters.

"Fuck. Yes."

I'm on a roll, words falling free, tumbling from my mouth. "Get your face between my thighs."

A rumble. "That's . . . holy . . . fucking . . . hot."

I don't stop. I don't want to stop. I say all the dirty words to him that I imagine saying to a lover. "I want to fuck your face. Please let me fuck your face."

"Jesus Christ." His groan is deep and carnal.

"Faster. Harder. Yes, like that. Oh God, just like that."

I'm not even touching myself. I'm not getting off. I'm simply speaking, but something rattles loose in me. I'm finally saying these words out loud, not in my head, and it's astonishing. A new aftershock of pleasure rushes over me as I let my fantasies have a voice, giving them sound and volume. "I want to come on your face."

He's silent. Dead silent, and I fear I've crossed a line.

"Gabe. Are you okay?"

"I'm. Great." His voice is sandpaper. "All that stuff you said—is that what you say in your head when you're touching yourself?"

"Yes. Is that weird? Is it too much?"

He lets out a long exhale. "That is the sexiest thing any woman anywhere has ever said."

A smile spreads of its own accord, and my skin feels as if it's glowing. "It is?"

"It so fucking is, and you need to be able to say all that when you're actually having sex."

"You really think I should say those things with someone else?"

"I guarantee that if you do, you will drive any man out of his mind with pleasure."

Right now, I want that man to be him.

24

ARDEN

The next morning as I stroll through the town square on the way to work, I feel like everyone's eyes are on me. Like they can see through me, an X-ray woman revealing all her risqué thoughts to the world on black-and-white film.

But no one stares, since all these wild, wonderful images are flicking by in my brain, only for me — images and sounds and memories of the things I said to Gabe, and that he said to me.

It was only the start of our sex education plan, and yet last night was not an experience that I can easily let go of. Nor do I want to. I feel alive and electric, like I'm living in a fevered dream.

Anticipation camps out in my chest as I near the firehouse. My heart ticks faster, and my wish to see him — to wave, to say hello — grows more intense.

But at the same time, I'm not sure how I should behave.

Everything feels a little different between us, even though we didn't cross any lines.

We didn't touch. We simply said racy words. But in saying them, I revealed myself. I showed him my wants, and now he knows some of my deepest desires.

I'm not only Arden, his Words with Friends pal and bowling buddy. I'm a woman who has after-dark wishes.

I know more of him too. I know how he approaches sex and women and experimentation.

It's like we're walking the tightrope of friendship, balancing precariously and tipping ever closer to the edge.

But as I pass the firehouse, my heart sinks. The truck is gone, and its absence reveals to me how badly I wanted to see him. I let out a long exhale that's tinged with more disappointment than I expected. Plus, he has a twenty-four-hour shift today, so there won't be any experiments tonight. But we're seeing each other tomorrow, and I'm debating whether I want to practice biting, spanking, or stripping, or if we can work in that elevator arms-in-the-air agenda item.

Later in the day, my phone pings with a text.

Gabe: Hey! Wild Care says Hedwig is recuperating nicely.

I punch the air in triumph. His note makes me happy in a whole new way. For the owl and also, I'm realizing, for *us*. Because we're normal. We can be owl-rescuers, and bowling buddies, and pizza friends, and coach and sex-thlete, and just . . . well, *friends*.

Good friends.

Arden: Yay! Also, you checked on Hedwig? I love that.

Gabe: Of course. I wanted an update, and I knew you'd want to know as well. So I checked on our owl.

Arden: Can I still adopt him? There's a high shelf in my store that I know he'd love.

Gabe: I'm sure Henry and Clare would LOVE his company.

Arden: Admit it. A bookstore owl would be so cool.

Gabe: Yes, it would be. But Hedwig belongs in the wild. Speaking of shelves, how's that one that you were worried was a little loose? Need me to take a look at it?

My heart beats a little faster from his offer, his willingness to help me. I head over to the shelf in question, rapping on it.

Arden: I checked it. All good!

Gabe: You know where to find me if you need anything.

Arden: Same to you. :)

This man does so much for me, and I only wish I could do something special for him. That afternoon, as I help a customer find an old Dashiell Hammett novel, I know precisely what that is.

25

GABE

"And that's some of what we do in an average day. Now, I'm wondering"—I tap my chin, surveying the eager crowd—"is there any chance any of you have any questions? I know it'd be pretty unusual for a first-grader to have questions. But you all should feel free to hit me up if you do."

A dozen little hands shoot in the air, and there's laughter from the grown-ups too. I spend the next twenty minutes answering questions here at the fire station. Most of the questions—surprise, surprise—involve the truck and the truck. Also, the truck.

When the questions ebb, I drop plastic fireman hats on the kids' heads and thank them for coming. The camp counselor also thanks me.

As the kids wander down the street back to the community center, Shaw emerges from the firehouse, gesturing to the troop. "Over-under on how many you scared away from the fire service on account of being so ugly?"

I screw up the corner of my lips as if I'm considering his question. "Hmm . . . I'd say at least a half dozen. But that still makes you the leader, since you scare them all off when you give the demos."

He runs a hand over his jaw. "Please. I'm like the goddamn superhero of every little aspiring firefighter in the country. They all want to be me when they grow up."

I park my hands on my hips. "Is that so? Do the kids have a secret shrine to you somewhere at their school?"

"Of course they do." He narrows his eyes. "So do the teachers, right in the teachers' lounge. They all have pictures of me from the fireman calendar on every wall."

"In your dreams."

"Why do you think they're all asking me to do demos? They love me and my scar."

I crack up. "You have such a rich fantasy life."

He grabs the hem of his shirt and shakes his hips, pretending to dance. "You're just jealous, Harrison. Admit it. I've got it going on." Lifting the shirt, he drags a hand over the faded scar that cuts across his hip, the mark that he definitely doesn't show at demos to kids here or in schools.

"Because you moonlight as a stripping fireman?"

Even though he does nothing of the sort, he mimes tossing out dollar bills. "I make it rain. Look at my hips. They don't lie." He shakes them as if he's a master dancer.

"What the hell do you actually do in your spare time?"

He pretends to zip his lips.

I shake my head. "Buddy, I am so sorry."

"What are you sorry for?"

"That you suffer from so many delusions."

He laughs, then his expression turns serious, his zany side slinking away. "Hey, did you hear about Charlie?"

"Yeah. I'm going to miss him." Charlie is moving back to Florida.

"Says he can't afford living here anymore. That's the tough part of being in California. This place is crazy expensive."

"It sure as hell is." I point from him to me. "And we are so damn lucky that we can do what we do, and not have to worry about where every cent is coming from or going to."

"That's the truth." Shaw is some kind of wizard financially and set himself up with several well-timed stock trades over the years so he wouldn't have to make tough choices and he wouldn't have to leave his hometown. He made enough wise investments that he was able to pursue this career and live in a town with ridiculous home prices at the same time. "I don't know that I can live someplace else. I love my sister, and I love my family too much."

I admire that about Shaw—he's a family man.

But when he mentions his sister, I don't think of Perri. I think of another person, one who's close with Perri.

Arden.

The woman I can't stop thinking about.

The woman who's uncovering a brazen new confidence about her wants and wishes.

She's speaking her mind, voicing her desires, and it's hot as hell.

And while I don't have any secret wants or wishes to share with the guys, it wouldn't be such a bad idea, either, to let the boys at work know I give a shit about them. I spend much of my time messing with them, as they do with me. But moments like this matter too. The honest ones. Because the fact is, I depend on them every day. I rely on Shaw to have my back, and he does the same with me.

"Hey, Shaw?"

He gives a quizzical lift of his brow. "Yeah?"

"You're a good guy. I'm glad we're on the same team."

He shoots me a *you have to be kidding me* look. "Have you gone all soft and fuzzy inside?"

I decide to own it. "Yeah, I have in this second. I'm going to miss Charlie when he leaves. Practically felt like he worked right here with us."

"He pretty much did."

"And you know what? I'd miss you if you left too, so I'd really like it if you'd stick around."

He smiles, and it's a genuine one. "You're stuck with me, Harrison. I'm not going anywhere."

"Let's keep it that way. Let's keep doing this—looking out for each other."

He offers a fist for knocking. "Sounds like a deal."

Shoes click behind me, and Shaw turns toward the sound then wiggles his eyebrows at me. "I believe you have a visitor."

I spin around, and I try to hide the smile, but it's no use. I can't help but grin when I see Arden. Lovely and gorgeous, bright and brainy Arden walking my way.

"Jesus Christ, Casanova. Just ask her out once and for all," Shaw says in a low voice.

"All in due time." And I will. As soon as we're done with her experiment. Which means the time will be sooner rather than later.

When she reaches us, she says hi to both Shaw and me, and I do my damnedest to rein in a ridiculous grin because, hell, am I ever happy to see her.

26

GABE

Shaw tips his chin at the woman in front of us. "Hey, Arden. Gabe and I had a little bonding session. Did you know he's all soft and sweet inside?"

Arden smiles. "Is that so?"

Shaw punches my stomach. "He's a total teddy bear. He was telling me that I'm his best friend."

I roll my eyes. "You're such a dick. I'll go back to telling you that you're a dick. Now get out of here, you dick."

"Nope. I'm not a dick. You love me. You fucking love me."

"I love it when you leave. See you, man."

He salutes us. "I'll let you two lovebirds catch up."

Arden raises an eyebrow as he heads back into the station. "Why did he say 'lovebirds'?"

"I cannot account for anything that knucklehead does." I hope that little white lie does the trick.

She exhales as if she's erasing Shaw from her head. "Dashiell Hammett. I know what your grandpa was talking about with the schnauzer."

She shows me a paperback—*The Thin Man* by Dashiell Hammett.

I give her a questioning look.

Her face brightens more. "The two married detectives have a dog. A *female schnauzer* named Asta. In the movie, the dog was changed to a male wire fox terrier. You said your pops liked hard-boiled detective books." Her smile radiates as she keeps going. "I don't think he was misremembering his collies. I think he was talking about this book when he was telling you about a female schnauzer. He was saying he wanted the female schnauzer because he didn't like that the dog had been changed from the book. That's what he was meaning."

The cogs turn in my head, clicking into place. A sense of wonder bordering on awe spreads through me as she solves the puzzle of his strange dog comments that weren't so strange after all. "That was it. Holy smokes. I think you're right."

Smiling, she hands the paperback to me. "It's a gift for him. From me to him."

My heart kicks around in my chest. I want to tell her that this detective work makes me fall a little more for her, because this means so damn much to me. I don't say those words exactly. Instead, I tell her in a way that shows how much she matters.

"Would you like to come with me tomorrow and give it to him yourself?"

Her eyes light up like sparklers. "I would love to meet your pops."

27

GABE

I've never brought a woman to see my grandfather before.

No need. No reason. It's not exactly where you go on a date, and I haven't been serious enough with anyone to bring her around. These visits—they're a family thing.

As we turn down the fifth-floor hallway, my shoulders tighten, and I stretch my neck, trying to loosen up. I'm glad I haven't run into Darla today, though, and I hope it stays that way.

Arden tells me she has to stop in the restroom, and I point in the direction of the elevators. "Right over there."

She doubles back, and I watch her turn the corner, then I lean against the wall, telling myself to relax.

When she joins me a minute or two later, I reach for her arm and meet her gaze. "Listen, he has good days and bad days. I never know which it'll be. That's the thing about walking into his suite—it's a little like answering a call. You hope for the best, but sometimes it's the worst." I take a breath, bracing myself for an eventuality. "Well, it hasn't quite been the worst yet, but someday it will be."

She nods, her big brown eyes filled with understanding. "That makes sense. There's a great unknown factor to what he's going through."

"Sometimes he's in another place entirely. Another time . . ."

"Does he know you?"

I swallow roughly. "He still does. I'm grateful for that. Sometimes he thinks it's another year, or that my grandmother is still alive."

"That's hard for everyone." She offers a small smile, keeping her eyes locked on mine. "Tell me what you want me to do or say if that happens."

My breathing steadies, and it's because of her, how calm she is, how she's not weirded out by any of this. "Just be yourself. I try to talk to him like I talk to anyone, and I remind him of when and where he is if he doesn't seem to know."

"That's easy. I can do that. *We* can do that."

I breathe a big sigh of relief. She's a natural with people. She knows how to talk to anyone, how to meet a person on his or her level without talking down or looking too far up. She's an eye-to-eye, face-to-face person.

We reach his suite, and the nerves quell a little

bit more. I take a steadying breath and say a prayer that it's a good day. After I knock, I walk in with Arden by my side.

Pops is parked on the couch, his gray hair neatly combed, his reading glasses perched at the end of his nose, peering into a book—*101 Places to See Before You Die*.

My heart leaps into my throat, tightening like a fist around it. I hate that last word, and I hate, too, that he likely won't see any of those places. "You have a new book, Pops?"

He looks up. "Emily gave it to me the other day."

And we're back in time. The fist tightens harder, gripping my heart. Arden takes my hand and squeezes it.

"You mean she gave it to you a few years ago?" I remind him gently.

He scrunches his wrinkled forehead. "She said we should check out some of these places sometime." He sets the book down and stares at Arden with hard eyes. "Is she a new nurse? A new aide?"

He doesn't like it when the rotation changes unexpectedly on him.

I shake my head, smiling. "This is my friend Arden."

His ruler-straight mouth shifts to a grin. He stands, smiles, and extends a hand.

Arden walks over and takes it. "Hello. I'm Arden East."

"Michael Sullivan, and you are a lovely lady.

Gabe's mentioned you a few times." He flashes me a devilish grin. "You're the one he thinks is quite pretty."

What was I thinking? My pops knows nearly everything. I am a great and complete idiot, because he has the power to spill all. I hope to hell he doesn't give her the keys to figure out what's going on in my heart.

But on the plus side, he seems fully present now.

Arden simply smiles. "Thank you so much. But the problem is, Gabe never mentioned to me how handsome his pops is. Do you think he was holding that back on purpose?"

My grandpa winks at her. "I think I'm falling too."

Too.

I told him she was special, but I never told him I was falling. I'm going to pretend he didn't say the word *too*. Or the word before it. *Falling.*

But in my head, I can't pretend, because it tugs at me. It feels like a whisper of the impending truth. Like I'm heading in that dangerous direction. I'm no idiot—I know I have Feelings for her with a capital F—but in the last few days they've grown stronger, more intense. Maybe they are cruising into Falling Town, and we all know where that road leads.

I'm going to pray that my pre-visit prep with Arden will keep Pops from spilling the beans.

He wiggles his brow then pats the couch. "Sit. Join me." He looks at me as I grab the chair across from them. "Gabe, why didn't you ever bring your girlfriend here before? She's much prettier to look at than you."

Girlfriend. He's going to kill me. "You are such a dirty dog, Pops."

Arden laughs and turns to him again. "Do you think he takes after you, Michael?"

He chuckles. "I had a way with the ladies. One in particular. I miss her so." Now he's most definitely in the present.

Arden seizes the opportunity, tapping his book. "I love this book. Where have you been? Where do you want to visit most?"

"So many places. I've been all over America. Been to Mexico. To Alaska. But after reading, I think I'd like to go to one of those ice hotels. Mostly, I want to see if it's as crazy as it sounds."

"It does sound nuts, doesn't it? Every time I read about one, I shiver inside. Do you feel that way?"

"That's exactly how I feel. Maybe I ought to focus on traveling to Fiji since it's so much warmer."

"You could get a hut on the ocean and read or fish all day long."

His blue eyes light up, and he's more animated than he's been in ages. "I'd go to Thailand next and try the street food."

"Have you seen the entry on Morocco? There's an entire city in that country called the Blue City. Everything—all the walls, all the buildings—is blue." She takes the book and flips through the pages, finding the entry and showing it to him.

He smiles then looks up at me, speaking in a faux stage whisper. "I think your girlfriend wants you to take her to the Blue City."

"I'll have to look into it."

He turns his focus back to Arden. "You're the bookstore lady?"

"Yes, I am. In fact, I brought you a book today." Dipping her hand into her purse, she gives him the Dashiell Hammett.

He chuckles. *The Thin Man*. Can you believe they changed the dog for the movie?"

"I simply cannot."

He flips to the opening chapter and reads the first few words. "*I was leaning against the bar in a speakeasy on Fifty-Second Street . . .*" He stops to look up from the pages. "I bet it'd sound prettier if you read it."

"I thought you'd never ask."

As she reads, I realize bringing her here might be both the greatest and dumbest thing I've ever done. As he asks for more and she keeps reading, my heart free-falls with every word. She never stops, never wavers. She does all the voices and reads another chapter, and then *just one more chapter*, each time he asks.

My heart spins faster in her direction, and I so badly want to tell her everything he's said about her feels true. I am falling for her, and I absolutely know what I'm falling into.

When he declares he's tired, we stand to leave, and Arden gives him a peck on the forehead.

"You come back now. I want Emily to meet you."

He's lost again. *Oh, Pops.*

I jump in. "I wish Nana could meet her too. But she can't, since she's not here anymore."

He sighs. "Oh."

"I love you." I give him a hug.

As we leave the suite, Arden squeezes my shoulder. "He's so wonderful."

"He's a great man. He came to all my games in high school. Many in college too."

"What about the majors?"

"He came to most of those as well. That was before . . ." My voice trails off. I collect myself. "He was there for my first save and my last one in the majors."

"He loves you so."

"The feeling is completely mutual." I shoot her an apologetic smile. "Sorry for all that girlfriend stuff."

She shakes her head. "Don't apologize. It's fine. I understand completely."

A small stone climbs up my chest, burrowing and pushing painfully. She understands because it's plausible that he messed up the fact.

The stone wedges against my lungs, and it hurts like a lie. I don't want to throw him under the bus. I don't want to use his fading memory as a parachute for the fact that I don't know how to tell her that what I feel for her is so much more than friendship.

But I'm not sure now is the time and place to tell her either. Nor do I want her to think I'm taking advantage of her when she's come to me for help.

That time will come soon enough though. Today's the fourth day. And we haven't tried a fourth-day experiment yet.

I choose a slice of the truth, serving it up like a small piece of pie. "I did tell him about you."

"You did?" Her voice rises, sounding hopeful.

"I told him what you meant to me. And I might possibly perhaps have mentioned how pretty you are."

Her smile is majestic. "Thank you."

That's all I say. I'm not lying, nor am I blaming him for twisting my words.

When we reach the elevator, I wish I could twist my words into a new truth. I wish she was with me and I could wrap my arms around her, kiss her forehead, and tell her how much more I want to mean to her.

But this will have to do for now. All the sex talk between us has muddied the waters, even though bringing her here today has made my heart clearer.

When the doors open, more clarity arrives.

It's in the form of her wishes. Her desires. Her secret fantasies.

There's something she wants, and I can give that

to her. I shift gears in another direction entirely, toward her list and perhaps something we can explore today.

The second the doors close, I know we have very little time. Maybe fifteen seconds. I meet her eyes. "What do you know? We're in an elevator."

She nibbles on her lower lip. "Yes, we are."

We're both in the same moment, talking the same language.

"Time for a lesson? We only have a few more days," I say.

"Let's make the most of it."

I step closer, take her wrists in my hands, and lift them above her head in one fast move. I push her against the wall. She lets out the sexiest sound I've ever heard, a sensual cross between a gasp and a murmur.

"*Ohhhh.*" She juts out her hips, a beautiful fucking invitation. I move closer, reading her every step of the way. Her eyes, shining with desire. Her lips, parted. Her chin, raised.

She nods, giving me permission to raise her arms higher, press harder. I align my body with hers as the car whisks down.

Her brown eyes are hazy. "I love this," she whispers.

"You really ought to be kissed into oblivion in an elevator . . . and by someone who knows how." I lean my body into hers, and a heady whimper falls from her lips. She must know how aroused I am. My hips press against her. She wriggles against me.

My mouth is inches from her delicious lips. We are hovering, poised in a moment when all these lessons could fly out the window and this could turn into a real kiss. A hot kiss. A hungry kiss.

I know she wants it.

Trouble is, I don't know if she wants it from me —or to learn how it feels.

But I don't know that I'm going to find the answer right now, so instead of searching for it, I take another liberty. Letting go of her wrists, I unclip her hair. The lush blonde strands fall through my fingers as I press a kiss to her neck. She *moans*.

She moans my goddamn name.

"Gabe."

I nearly die of an overdose of desire. I nip her neck, and she murmurs. Everything between us could change in an instant. She could turn her face to me. I could bring mine closer to her. Our lips could brush together.

I bite her neck, and she's groaning now, practically melting against my body.

Everything could change if I moved my lips.

One kiss and we'd no longer be playing games.

The moment expands into choices, a cascade of options that all entice me.

But those choices end when the car stops. The elevator doors open on the first floor. We separate, and I see Darla.

28

ARDEN

The redheaded nurse is fresh-faced, with glowing skin and clear blue eyes. But she gives us a clinical once-over, and it's as if I've been caught stealing meds from the pharmacy closet.

The way she stares is knowing, as if she's adding up the clues.

My hair is down, a little wild.

Yet my hair wasn't down when I ran into her in the fifth-floor ladies' room when I first arrived.

Does she know I was about to be kissed senseless in the elevator seconds ago? Does she know I was ready to wave the white flag of surrender and give in to all these wild feelings I have for my friend? She can't know that, of course. She doesn't know me.

But she knows him.

Her eyes flick to the man next to me, and she says his name in a businesslike manner. "Hi, Gabe."

Too businesslike.

His Adam's apple bobs, almost painfully, it seems, as he swallows. "Hi, Darla." His voice is strained.

"How's Michael? I trust he's well?" Her tone is chipper but forced.

"Having a good day."

"That's wonderful to hear." She raises her chin and casts a quick glance at me.

It doesn't take a detective to figure out the mystery.

My stomach churns as the answer clicks into place.

He dated her.

I don't know when. I don't know for how long. He never mentioned her, nor would I have expected him to do so. But he clearly did.

"This is Arden," he says, as if the words are new and strange on his tongue.

She raises her hand in a clinical wave. "Pleasure to meet you." She gestures down the hall. "I should get back to work. I'm glad everything is going well. Have a great day."

Darla's voice is professional as she turns on her heel, but beneath that veneer, I can make out all the undertones. I can hear everything unsaid.

She wanted to ask Gabe for more. He wasn't interested in more because that's who he is. He's the ladies' man. He's the charmer. That's exactly why I asked him for help.

But at this moment, his past cuts me. It makes me want to shut down, protect myself.

Yet, maybe this run-in is exactly what I need to remind me we can't be more. When he looks at me with fire in his eyes like he did in the elevator, like he did at the Garden of Eden, it's because he's remarkably good at sex and remarkably good at charming women.

Not because he's craving me the same way I'm longing for him. I want him in a way that's more than physical, in a way that's dancing scarily close to my heart.

I purse my lips, locking in emotions I don't want to set free.

I don't want to be her. I don't want to feel icy or cold toward him. I don't want him out of my life.

He means too much to me. I can't let my burgeoning emotions or my blooming libido lure me into situations that feel too risky, like a kiss. If we kiss, I'll fall into trouble. I'll lose control of my heart.

We continue out, and when we reach the parking lot, he clears his throat. "I'm sorry about that. I went out with her."

The admission of what I knew to be true still hurts. I try to shrug it off. "It's no big deal."

"It was only once."

The hurt goes deeper, because it's like he's justifying his one-and-done ways for my sake. "Gabe, it's fine." I rustle in my bag for my sunglasses because it's bright and because I need to hide my eyes from him.

"I didn't feel anything for her," he adds, and it's too much. Too much to know he can connect with a woman without feeling a thing.

I hold up a hand. "There's no need to justify anything to me."

He grabs my wrist—like he did in the elevator but without desire, only determination. "I'm not justifying it."

"Then what are you doing?"

"Jesus Christ, I'm explaining why things were weird. Would you just let me?"

"They weren't weird, and you don't owe me an explanation. I didn't ask for your help in the bedroom because I thought you were innocent. I asked for help because you have lots of experience."

His jaw clenches, ticking. "That's not the point, Arden. I didn't have sex with her. We didn't do anything."

"It doesn't matter," I say again, but my voice is tight, stretched thin as I force out untrue words. It does matter. Everything matters. If I let this longing between us spiral into uncharted waters, I'll be the next one he passes on the street and shares an awkward introduction with. The next woman who's professional and polite with him.

"Yes. It. Does." He lets go of my wrist and drags a hand through his hair. "Will you just listen to me?"

I exhale, my throat catching, and I nod. The least I can do is give him the floor.

He holds up his index finger. "We went on one date. Nothing happened. She wanted to go out again. And I didn't. I told her as much. I was upfront and clear. I didn't lead her on about my intentions. And I didn't screw her and ditch her. I'm sorry she was kind of cold."

"It's okay. I'd probably feel the same way she did," I say, letting down my guard, choosing honesty.

"I don't want you to feel like that."

How do you want me to feel? I'm dying to ask. *How do you feel?* Because something changed in the elevator. Something shifted between us. And I don't know what it is or how to go forward. But if this brief experiment with him has taught me anything, it's that speaking my mind matters. "I want to be friends with you. I don't want to be the woman who gives you a cold look because you didn't want to go out again. And I'm sorry," I say, choking out an apology.

"For what?"

"For the 'experience' comment. It was snide and shitty."

He laughs. "It's okay. You called a spade a spade."

I shake my head. "It was rude."

"I didn't feel slut-shamed, for what it's worth."

"Good. I don't believe in slut-shaming."

"Then we practice the same religion. There

should be no such thing as slut-shaming. Sex is good. Sex is a wonderful thing. Let's stop arguing."

I nod, swallowing the dumb lump in my throat. "I hate fighting."

He reaches for me, wraps his arms around my shoulders, and tugs me close. "Then let's not fight."

I rest my head against his shoulder, savoring the strength of his arms, the warmth of his touch. But even so, I'm still thinking about how his arms felt in the elevator. How his hands pinned my wrists. How his body moved against mine, hard and aroused.

And I'm thinking, too, about how I feel when I'm with him. How I felt walking down that hallway with him to see his pops, like I was special to Gabe. How I felt in the suite when the three of us talked, and then when I read. I swear Gabe looked at me like he was seeing new things in me.

I think I'm seeing new things in him too.

That's so damn dangerous.

But even after seeing what happens to women who want more of Gabe than he can give, I still long for both parts of him.

For the man who hugs me like this.

And the one who wanted me like that.

I want both sides, and I wonder if I can find a way to have them without getting hurt. And without losing something as precious as our friendship.

29

GABE

My mom's chicken tacos are delicious, and my father insists she not lay a finger on the dishes when we're done feasting.

"Go sit in your new porch swing, read a book, put your feet up." He points to the wraparound deck, home to the wooden swing she loves. "I don't want to see you in the kitchen at all, Maggie."

She huffs, raising her hands in surrender. "If you insist."

"I absolutely do."

I pat my dad on the back. "Don't worry, Mom. I'll make sure he doesn't slack off in the kitchen and resort to watching baseball."

"Like you would do," my dad teases.

"I know you'll both be good boys," she says then excuses herself.

I join my father, helping him clean as we catch up on the latest news—Charlie leaving for Florida, my sister getting ready for her third kid, and, of course, Pops.

"I heard you and Arden visited Michael this morning." There's a leading tone to his voice as he hands me a plate to dry.

"Did Mom tell you that?"

He laughs. "Nope. Michael did. I stopped by to go for a walk with him this afternoon, and all he talked about was the two of you. I swear, he never shut up. He was quite taken by her."

I set the plate in the cupboard. "He has good taste."

"Indeed." Dad clears his throat, raises his eyebrows. "You've never brought anyone by before. Not even Shaw or Charlie."

"I know."

"What's so special about Arden?" The question is open-ended, rather than an interrogation. It's designed for conversation.

But I've told him about Arden. "You know she's special."

"Tell me why again."

It's easy to go on about why she's captured my attention. "She's smart, and she's loyal, and she has no problem kicking my ass in darts or bowling or puzzles. And she's kind to other people. To all people, as a matter of fact. She makes me laugh. And she's pretty damn straightforward." I flash back to earlier in the parking lot, and the words we said. We skirted around the topic at first, but in the end, she was up-front with me, especially about her wishes—being friends.

"What are you going to do about all that?"

I grab another plate and run a towel across it. "That's the issue. She's focused on the friend zone, it seems. So what the heck can I do?"

He chuckles thoughtfully. "Keep showing her what a good friend you can be. Let her know that's rock solid. There's no better foundation for something serious later on than a friendship right now."

"Is that so?"

"That is so. I should know. Your mom and I were friends first. And I wore her down."

I laugh. "You're relentless. Like erosion."

"Exactly. That's how I won her over. Like a river over rocks." He hangs up the towel on the cupboard knob and pins me with his serious stare. "I'm not saying Arden will fall for you. She may be one of the rare women immune to your charms."

"Ha. Ha. Ha."

"But if you think she's not there yet, all you can do is keep showing her you're there for her."

I let his advice roll around in my head as we leave the kitchen and tune into the Giants, but after a half inning, I'm restless, and my mind is elsewhere. My mind is on her. I take out my phone and open Words with Friends, returning to a game we started a few days ago.

Neither one of us has played a word for a while, so I text her first.

Gabe: How's your night? Just had dinner with my parents. You should join us sometime soon.

That's erosion. The good kind.

Arden: I'd love to. :)

There. Something to build on. I scan the board, hunting for a word to ladder onto. I laugh privately when I spot something I can form on the *T* at the end of another word.

Gabe: Does "catdoor" count as a word?

Arden: There is no universe in which "cat door" is a word. It is two words. You sneak. :)

Gabe: New words are made all the time. You never know. Let me try to play it.

And I try, but of course the game rejects me.

Gabe: Fine, you were right. But I have other words to make. TREAT.

She plays another word quickly.

Arden: WRIST.

That makes me think of one thing only. And it's not a friendly thing.

Gabe: By the way, did you like having your wrists pinned above your head in the elevator?

Arden: I think you know the answer to that.

Gabe: I think I do. And I hope you know the answer to the corollary.

Arden: The corollary being whether you liked it?

Gabe: Yes.

Arden: I do know the answer. You liked it.

Gabe: No, I fucking loved it.

Arden: Me too.

I form another word, using the *S* in wrist.

Gabe: STRIP.

Arden: Are you trying to tell me something?

Gabe: I believe I am.

Yep. I'm not following my dad's advice at all. I'm not being friendly in the least. But then again, I want her to see me as more than a friend. And she's clearly playing along.

She takes her turn, playing off the *T* in STRIP.

Arden: TEA.

As I stare at her letters, another note from her pops up.

Arden: I don't have an *S* or an *E*. But I think you get my meaning. The word I want to form is TEASE.

Gabe: I do get your meaning. And I like your meaning. Are you still game for it?

Arden: Yes, and I promised you dinner and coconut bars.

I want the dinner, I want the coconut bars, I want the apron, I want the striptease, and I want her. All of her. At the end of her research project, I don't want to be in the friend zone anymore. I want to be in the everything zone, and perhaps I'll find my way there when her clothes come off.

Gabe: Name the time and place, and what I can bring to the dinner.

Arden: Are you off tomorrow night?

Gabe: Till midnight. Graveyard shift calls my name.

Arden: Can you be here at seven?

Gabe: What should I bring?

Arden: You.

It's only a text. I can't read any emotion into it. But I swear the way she writes that one word lights a fire inside me.

30

ARDEN

Vanessa implores me with Puss-in-Boots eyes as we stand outside Happy Days. "Promise me something, Arden."

"What is it?"

She grabs my hands, grips my fingers tight. "Whatever I say in there, whatever I do, don't let me buy anything."

Laughing, I answer, "I promise."

She issues a command. "Solemnly swear."

Letting go of hers, I raise my right hand. "I swear I will hold you back, just as I swear the book is always better than the movie, no matter what."

"Bless you. You're a true friend." She swings open the door to her favorite vintage shop in neighboring Hope Falls, where we've slipped away for a quick lunchtime shopping break. "This store has the best stuff. I snagged this dress last week on sale." She sways her hips, showing off the white swing dress with its peach pattern. The ensemble is capped with sparkly orange shoes.

"Wherever did you get those there's-no-place-like-home heels?"

"They're my if-the-Wicked-Witch-of-the-East-liked-orange-instead-of-red ruby slippers." She gestures to the heels. "Also, I found them online after an hour of bargain hunting for incredible shoes."

That's her favorite pastime, and she excels at it.

We head into the shop, and I'm swimming in a sea of retro style. Tea-length dresses, flouncy skirts, twinsets, and so many patterns: light-blue dresses bursting with cherry designs; rockabilly skirts made of pink-and-white gingham; and blouses with flamingo designs, checked prints, and embroidered pineapples.

"Gah, I want it all," Vanessa whispers, making grabby hands at the clothing treasures.

I clasp her wrists. "Shhh. It's going to be okay. We mustn't let you short circuit."

She wriggles away, her arms shooting out robotically as she walks, trance-like, to a mint-green dress with a typewriter-key pattern across the bodice. Next to it is a skirt with cartoonish images of books on it.

I yank her over to me, spinning her around. "You made me promise to make you resist."

"Resistance is futile. I can't do it." She throws one hand on her forehead as if she's fainting.

I relent, since I know the trick to keeping her on track. "Fine, get the dress."

She snaps me a look. "You're an enabler."

I gesture to my face. "Then enable *me* instead."

She nods crisply, snapping out of it, refocusing on her shopping mission. "You're right. I'm a personal shopper today," she says, as if it's a mantra she needs to remind herself of. *Mission accomplished.* "Do you want that green skirt?"

I laugh. "It's adorable, but today we are here for an apron."

"Right. Let me find you a sexy apron, then."

We head to a rack near the dressing rooms, where Vanessa sorts through short aprons and cute aprons and boob-boosting aprons.

I touch a satiny red one then the air, making a sizzling sound. "Hot damn."

"Aprons are the new lingerie."

"You're telling me." I point to one that has a heart-shaped neckline.

"That's hella sexy." She quirks an eyebrow. "And I bet looking that sexy will make you feel hella sexy. So how exactly are you going to answer the door like that and not want to make hot fireman babies with him?"

"It's just practice," I insist, since I need the reminder. "All we're doing is practice."

She hums, seemingly unconvinced. "You know what they say about practice."

"Practice makes perfect?"

"No. They say practicing answering the door in a sexy apron leads to . . ." She mimes a drumroll. "Sex."

"I don't think that's a saying."

"But it should be. Especially in your case." A note of warning sounds in her tone.

"It'll be fine. We're committed to friendship first," I say, trying to stay strong.

But inside, I wonder briefly if she's right. Each day I do want more and more with Gabe. Every time I see him, the longing grows more intense, the desire stronger. But our friendship matters too much to risk simply for dumb, pesky hormones.

I want to believe it's merely hormones at play.

Trouble is, I can't quite buy that line of reasoning anymore. Try as I might, when my logical brain feeds that to me, my heart seems to stick out its tongue at my head then laugh.

Because my heart, my God, it somersaults when he's near me. It does that *shimmy shimmy bang bang*, even when I think of him and who he is as a man. The way he takes care of his pops, of the owl, his friends, and all the people he doesn't know—the strangers he helps every day. How he gives his mom books and makes time for dinner with his parents. They say you can learn all you need to know about a man from how he treats his mom, and Gabe treats Mama Harrison with love, respect, and devotion.

All the chambers in my heart are hammering right now.

And I need to be careful because today is about aprons and research and fantasies. It's not about silly dreams that can't come true.

Dreams I don't entirely understand.

I shove them aside, kicking them to a compartment in the back of my mind.

"Ooh! This one!" Vanessa thrusts a black apron in my direction. The little skirt is covered in tiny white dots, and the neckline sports a soft fuchsia bow. "It's hot—covers the boobs, and a little bit of leg—and it's so very you." She presses it against me. "You're going to look delectable."

I turn to the mirror, loving what I see. "It is indeed hella sexy."

She squeezes my shoulder. "Also, listen. Maybe you should consider whether there's something more happening between the two of you. Don't you think?"

"He's not into me like that."

She shoots me a steely stare. "But are *you*? Are you like that? Are you liking this pretend thing?"

So much.

I like it so much I can't jam all these feelings inside me. They're bursting, jostling to break free. I sweep my gaze side to side, then whisper, "Yesterday, he pinned my arms above my head in an elevator. Pressed his body against mine. Bit my neck."

She fans her face. "I'm getting hot just thinking about it. How was it?"

"One of the most intense things I've ever experienced. The other night I practiced dirty talk on the phone with him."

"And?"

I fan my face this time.

"Sounds like the line between practice and performance is getting thinner."

I draw a deep breath. "I know."

"So you're doing this, then? The whole apron thing?"

The idea still ignites me. "Yes."

She exhales deeply, pushing all the air in the world from her lungs. "You're a brave and bold woman." She snags the apron from me and marches to the counter. "This one's on me."

A few minutes later, we meet Perri for lunch at a nearby diner. Over iced tea and salads, Vanessa fills her in on my apron purchase, and I repeat the elevator story.

I repeat it because . . . it feels good to say it. Because I like sharing it with them. Most of all, I love the way I relive it with a fresh rush of sensations over my skin. A brand-new wave of tingles. It's like I'm having the moment again and again. And the moment feels good in so many ways—heart, mind, and body.

Perri reaches for her handcuffs and dangles them before me. "Here. Take these tonight. You'll need them."

A blush creeps across my cheeks. "I don't think I'm ready for cuffs yet."

She laughs. "They're not for you. You better handcuff Gabe to the mailbox, or he'll be all over you."

Vanessa smacks palms with Perri.

"Please. I can handle it," I say.

Vanessa arches a brow. "But can you? Can you handle it if he wants more than sex charades?"

My pulse quickens at the thought.

I raise my chin, playing it cool. "Of course. Just a few more days and we go back to the way we were."

Perri takes a sip of her iced tea, looking thoroughly unconvinced. "You really think you can snap your fingers and go back to being pals who bowl and throw darts?"

"As long as we don't cross any lines." I have to believe this.

Perri gives me a sympathetic smile. "Sweetie, I don't think it has to do with lines."

"What does it have to do with?"

She taps her sternum. "*This.*"

I don't want her to be right. Because *this*—my heart—is already fighting against my head.

31

ARDEN

When I devised the week-long plan, I figured that'd be all I'd need to shore up my skills.

Or, really, to develop the skills, but as I glance at the clock in the store that afternoon, I'm keenly aware that we have only a few days left to knock out the rest of my list.

Theoretically, we could go on indefinitely, but that's not fair to him, or me. The longer this goes on, the harder it will be to separate heart and head.

Besides, the whole point of this research project is so I have the skills for the next time a handsome man strides into my store and asks me out.

Or the next time I decide to ask a man out.

That's what I should be focused on — my newfound confidence. Not whether my best guy friend would slide out of the friend zone and into the romance zone with me.

Because . . . THAT WON'T HAPPEN.

Right now, though, the person coming into my store isn't a potential date, but the next meeting of one group of book club ladies. Miriam wanders in first, saying hello, followed by CarolAnn, Sara, and Allison.

They settle in, discussing a new book this time—Nora Roberts's *Year One*, an apocalyptic journey through a ravaged United States in the aftermath of a virus.

"Think about all the skills you would need at the end of the world," Sara says in her husky voice, peering at her crew over her cat-eye glasses as I reorganize the shelves.

Allison, of the nipple clamps, chimes in. "Exactly. What happens to me in an apocalypse? I'm a painter. It's not as if there's going to be any need for painters."

Miriam chuckles. "It makes you realize the value of experience. You actually have to get out and do things. Try things."

I slide some new travel books into the section on Denmark, battling Henry, who seems to think Copenhagen belongs next to Buenos Aires. He paws at *Ten Things to Do in Denmark*, and I gently remind him to keep his mitts in his own business. "Entirely wrong hemisphere," I tell the cat as Sara weighs in on this new world order.

"I'd have to learn all the things I don't know. I couldn't fake my way through it," she says. "I'd have to figure out how to fish. Learn how to catch my dinner in the river."

Miriam glances up and meets my eyes. "Arden, what do you think?"

I point to Sara. "I'm sticking with her in this scenario. Since I've no clue how to fish, and she seems determined to find dinner."

Miriam laughs. "See? Brains matter. Arden has a plan. Glom onto the fisherwoman."

"Clearly, there won't be a great need for bookstores or book clubs, but if you ladies are the survivors, I can also cook the fish for our little community," I offer.

Allison cracks up. "I like that approach. You have to be willing to roll up your sleeves and try all sorts of new things."

CarolAnn stares at Allison with curious eyes. "'Try new things' is your mantra."

Allison smiles like she has a secret. "I do like trying new things."

CarolAnn makes a rolling gesture with her hands as if to say *serve up the goods*. "Is this the moment you tell us about how you learned some crazy new position in bed, like you were telling us the other week when you tried the wheelbarrow?"

Miriam slaps her linen-clad thigh, and the book club ladies all slide back into their bawdy style, talking about what they'd do to pass the time at the end of the world. "Allison will be busy trying new things then," Miriam says.

Sara chimes in with, "After catching the fish and hunting for food, the only thing to do would be sex. There would be no cell phones."

"Don't look to me to repopulate though. I'm in menopause," Allison says, joined by a chorus of *Hear! Hear!*

As they chat about their apocalyptic sex plans, I take inventory not only of my shelves, but of my own plans.

Is it true that there's no substitute for experience? Can I really learn how to catch a fish by pretending to catch a fish?

A shiver runs up my spine as I think about the difference between pretending and reality.

I wonder how risky it would be to cross that line tonight.

Maybe it won't be too dangerous.

After all, if I can continue to keep *this*—my heart—under lock and key, I should be fine.

Perfectly fine.

* * *

That night, while the dinner I cook for Gabe warms in the oven, I take a shower, then dry my hair, brush some powder on my face, comb mascara on my eyelashes, and spread a new jasmine lotion up and down my smoothly shaven legs.

Am I really doing this?

I look in the mirror and take a deep breath, answering my own question.

I am doing this.

I grab the apron from my bed and wrap it around my waist then over my breasts, tying it at the neck. It covers me, but only barely. It's sinfully short and hits me mid-thigh. I slip on a pair of simple white panties, since I'm not ready to answer the door with nothing on beneath this scrap of frontal nudity–covering fabric.

I step into a pair of black heels and stare at my reflection again.

You are crazy.

But crazy has never felt so seductive or sensual. That's exactly how I look and precisely how I feel.

I do something else I've never done. I snap a sexy selfie, but it's not a full body shot. It's only a sliver of me, enough to show my thigh, the apron, and the tie around my waist.

It's an appetizer.

Feeling daring and loving it, I send it to him.

Seconds later, my phone pings with a text.

Gabe: It's now official. Let the record reflect, there is nothing sexier than an apron.

But what's sexier is the next note he sends.

Gabe: Allow me to amend that. Nothing sexier than an apron on you. And while I'm giving official pronouncements, I'll just add, so it's clear: I CAN'T FUCKING WAIT TO SEE THE REST OF IT.

A knowing smile spreads across my face. I can't wait for him to see it too.

Arden: I'm ready . . .

As I hit send, I let that word roll around my brain. *Ready.* I feel ready to answer the door. The food is cooked, the coconut bars are done, and now I'm going to live out a fantasy.

I'm not really sure why my fantasy has been to answer the door in an apron and little else. I think it's the sheer incongruity of the moment. The idea that a woman can be cooking and working and reading, and then do something entirely risqué.

She can completely floor her man.

As I return to the kitchen to check that everything's ready, I stop in my tracks like a cartoon character whacked into awareness by a frying pan.

Surprise.

I'm missing the element of surprise. I've already told him I'll be wearing an apron.

I've detailed this fantasy. I've delineated every step. I sent him a freaking photo, for crying out loud. There's no more mystery. There's no gift for him to unwrap.

But that's the fantasy—the surprise.

I want to witness the shock in his eyes.

I want to experience how his shock sends electricity shooting all over my body, reaching to every cell.

I want to stun him into . . . arousal.

When that stark truth hits my brain, I know I need to change my plans. I'm not sure what to do with all this desire, but I know what to do with the fantasy.

I scurry to my bedroom, untie the apron, and toss it onto the bed.

I slide off the cotton panties, rummage through my top drawer, and find something I bought for myself a few months ago. Something pretty, just for me.

A burgundy lace push-up bra, with matching low-rise panties.

That's it.

I put them on.

The doorbell rings.

32

ARDEN

My nerves skyrocket, but they're not only nerves. They're fluttering hummingbirds, zinging around inside me. They're desire, *my* desire to catch a fish rather than paint a fish.

I want the experience, all of it.

You can do this, I tell myself.

Then out loud, "I can do this."

With my head high, I walk to the door in my heels, a sway to my hips, feeling confident, feeling sexy.

I peer through the peephole, and my world goes whoosh.

I ache as I look at him.

He wears well-worn jeans and a light-blue shirt that shows off his strong biceps and ropy forearms. He's holding a bottle of sparkling white wine.

It goes well with a striptease, I told him the other night.

Through the peephole, I study him, and the tingles spread down my bare arms, because he looks like he wants to be here.

Only here.

Nowhere else.

There are no nerves in him, just some kind of wild hope, and I can feel that hope centered on me. At this moment, I *know*. He wants me the same way I want him.

Like we both wanted each other in the elevator.

What comes next?

I'm not sure of the answer.

But I'm sure of this new truth—that ache I feel isn't only sexual. It's a pull and a tug from deep inside me. Because of who he is, what he's been to me, what we've done. Not only for the last several days, but the last year. I long for him in so many ways, and I hardly know what to do with this explosion of awareness, with this burst of feelings for him. Wildly intense feelings that make me want so much more than a striptease.

I do what I can do.

The practical.

I can open the door.

I reach for the knob and turn it. It creaks, and here goes nothing. I open the door all the way, as ready as I'll ever be for the rest of the night to unfold, starting with my fantasy turned reality.

I glide one arm up the doorjamb so my hip juts

out, and I give him my best seductive housewife pout. "Hey there. Dinner is on the table."

He blinks and slides a hand across his stubbled jaw, as a strangled moan of appreciation slides past his lips.

His lips part, but he appears thoroughly incapable of words as his eyes travel up and down my body. Up and down, then back again, his gaze heating me up, sizzling my skin. After a few more tours of duty, he stops at my face, his baby blues shimmering with desire. "I'm ready for dinner. And for dessert."

His words come out hot and heavy, and the weight of them makes my pulse soar.

I gesture to my outfit. "I guess this meets your approval."

"This meets every seal of approval in the world."

I've never heard his voice sound so husky. The rasp in it feeds me. It moves through me, giving me another dose of confidence, another serving of naughtiness.

I bring my hand to my mouth, an exaggerated Betty Boop move. "Oh no! You were expecting me in an apron. Oops!" I raise a finger, the sign to wait. "I'll be right back."

I turn on my heels, giving him a view of my barely-covered derriere as I saunter back to my bedroom.

33

GABE

There's a fire extinguisher handy. I bought her extras a few months ago when I installed additional smoke alarms too.

Pretty sure they're going off right now.

Because I am *en fuego*.

That ass.

Those legs.

Those curves.

Yes, it's a five-alarm raging in my body as I stare, slack-jawed, at my good friend while she turns the corner into her bedroom.

Evidently, I'm still a gentleman since I don't go chase her in there. I wait, like a good boy. Or, really, like a dinosaur of the cock-a-saurus rex variety.

She's magnificent in all her nearly naked glory, and even though I was panting like a dog to see her in the apron, her switcheroo worked.

Hell, did it ever work. I tug at the neck of my

shirt. I try in vain to adjust myself in my jeans.

No luck. Her effect on me is stubbornly self-evident, and I'm damn sure I'm not going to be able to erase the image of her barely covered body from my brain any time soon.

Nor do I want to.

Shoes click against the hardwood floor, and she emerges, stopping at the end of the hallway, gesturing to her new ensemble. "Is this better?"

A small black apron covers her front and her belly, reaching down to mid-thigh.

I walk to her and take yet another liberty when I get there, running a hand down her bare arm. "Everything you wear looks amazing, and if you ever open the door in lingerie, or in this, whoever is lucky enough to be on the other side is going to be one happy motherfucker."

A slow smile spreads, and her eyes stay on mine. Like she doesn't want to look away.

"Thank you." Her words are soft and breathy, and they ghost across my skin, weaving around me. She takes my hand, squeezes. "I mean it, Gabe. *Thank you.* For all of this." She waves around at her house, and I furrow my brow.

"What do you mean?"

She takes a breath as if she's fortifying herself. "For letting me try new things."

My heart vaults out of my chest, skidding at her feet. "You don't have to thank me."

She swallows. "But I do. You're my friend, and

that means you make me feel safe, but somehow, you make me feel beautiful too. I don't know how you do it, but you do."

I close my eyes for a second, processing her words. It's no mystery to me why I make her feel beautiful. None whatsoever, but I need to demystify it for her, and soon.

I shake my head, trying to form words.

"What is it?" Her voice rises.

I take a breath, look at her again. It's hard to look away. "Thank you for trusting me to be the one you try new things with."

"There's no one else I'd want as a guide."

No one else.

The one.

That's what I want. For all her explorations to begin and end with me. "But there is one more thing you wanted to try, I believe?"

"What is that?" Curiosity weaves through her tone.

I make a circling gesture with my finger. "Turn around, Arden."

A wicked grin takes hold of her mouth and widens. She spins halfway.

I point to the living room wall. "Hands against the wall."

She bends forward, dipping into a beautiful, enticing L. I move behind her, sucking in a harsh breath through my teeth as I enjoy the peek at her ass, her cheeks barely covered by the lace panties.

"Ready?"

"So ready." A tremble moves through her body, and it's the most sensual thing I've ever seen. It's evidence, the physical manifestation of all I've been seeing in her eyes these last few days. A true and real desire. All I can think about is whether one quick slide of my hand to cup her between her legs would reveal if she's on the edge too.

But that's not what I said I'd do.

Instead, I raise my hand then lower it, swatting her ass.

"Oh!" she yelps.

I rub my hand over the flesh. "Did it hurt?"

She nods. "But do it again."

I laugh. "You little junkie."

I swat her other cheek then soothe it with my palm.

I'm so damn tempted to plant a kiss on those pink cheeks. To grab her luscious ass and squeeze hard. But this will have to suffice, and if I'm doing it right, I'll leave her wanting more.

I give one more swat then grab her waist, yank her up, and whisper, "Now feed me, woman."

And that tremble? It turns into a full-body shudder.

I don't know how the hell I'm going to make it through this meal.

* * *

I'm so sad.

I completely understand the sad panda saying now.

Because Arden is now dressed.

She's serving dinner in . . . wait for it . . . *clothes*.

Cue the tears.

But the chicken stir-fry she's made is heavenly, and I can't complain about her cooking.

I try to remember my dad's words—focus on the friendship. But now that I've seen her in a bra and panties—dear God, has a bra and pair of panties ever looked as good on a woman as they do on her? —I can't unsee it.

Can't unsee the apron either.

Can't unsee anything.

Nor can I unhear the *thank you*.

The vulnerability in her voice. The way she wanted me to know that what we've done—and not done—matters to her.

"Do you realize how useful you'd be at the end of the world?" she asks as she picks up the plates at the end of the meal.

I grab them from her and take them to the sink. "That's random. Why are you asking that?"

"You have real skills. You can put out fires *and* build them."

"You think I should become an arsonist at the end of the world?"

"I'm just thinking about the things the ladies at the book club said today." She turns on the faucet.

"What did they say?"

She tells me about the conversation, and her voice is pitched higher, and that's when it hits me. She's nervous.

I move in behind her and turn off the water. "Let's do the dishes later. Let's just sit and talk now."

"About the end of the world?"

I shake my head, grab the bottle of wine along with two glasses, and guide her out of the kitchen and to the living room. We sit on the couch.

"Tell me more about the ladies in the book club." I pour two glasses and hand her one. She loves talking about work, so this should ease her mind.

She takes a drink. "They're these bawdy sixty-somethings. They're funny and bold, but they're real too. They talk about how they feel and what they think. I love that they read everything from memoirs to romance to dystopian lit."

"Sounds just like you. You're an omnivore reader." I down some of the sparkling wine, and it tickles my tongue.

"That's true. Maybe that's partly why I connect with them. But I also do because of their friendships with each other. It reminds me of how I want to be in thirty years."

"You want to be a bawdy lady in a book club?"

She nods. "I do. I want the people I'm close with now to still be in my life. To still be part of my story."

Her meaning isn't lost on me. She's talking about

her girlfriends, but she's also talking about me. I'm not sure how to give her the reassurance she needs, so I keep it broad.

"You will be. I've no doubt about that. No one is writing anyone else out of their story."

She drinks some more, stares at the window looking thoughtful, then turns back to me. "Sometimes I want to ask the ladies for advice."

"What would you ask them?"

She lowers her voice to a feathery whisper. "If they think it's crazy that I want to do a striptease for my best guy friend."

I laugh, loving the direction she's heading. "I'll answer on their behalf."

"Will you now?"

"The answer is most decidedly no. It's not crazy."

She raises her glass, offering a toast. "To friendship. We can stay friends, right? Even if you see me in nearly nothing?"

"I want that badly." *To stay friends and to see her in nearly nothing.* The trouble is, I want a third thing too, but I've no idea if she does. I'm confident she's physically in the zone, but I don't know if her heart is hanging out even remotely in the same vicinity as mine.

She stands, sets down the glass, and tells me she'll be right back.

And because I know her, I don't turn on "Pour Some Sugar on Me" or "Back in Black." Grabbing my phone, I find Norah Jones on Spotify, because it's sexier, because it's mood music, and because I've heard her play it before.

I lean back against the couch, and soon her shoes echo against the floor. *Holy smokes.*

The pink dress is gone, and in its place is the black apron with the pink bow. But she's changed something else too. Her hair is pinned up high on her head in a clip, and she stops in front of me.

Jesus Christ. My throat is dry. Parched, even.

"Hi."

"Hi."

"Want a dance?"

"Fuck, yeah."

She turns around, raises her arms above her head, and sways.

That's all she does.

No gyrations. No twerking.

She moves her hips back and forth, but it's not a striptease. It's more like I'm looking through a peephole, witnessing a woman in her room, dancing alone, her eyes closed, music pulsing in her veins. This dance is more sensual and erotic than I imagined. It's like I've been invited into her private thoughts.

She leans her head back and runs her hands down her sides.

She's stunning. Her ass wiggles in front of me, but she's not going for an in-your-face-with-a-G-string move. She's simply grooving to the music.

"How's that?" she whispers, tossing her gaze

over her shoulder at me.

Our eyes connect, and in hers I see vulnerability and passion at the same damn time.

"It's so fucking sexy."

She smiles, and it's a new kind of smile. Daring and pleased. "Yeah?"

"Yeah."

Desire charges across my body in sharp, hot spikes as she turns around, bends forward, and places her hands on my knees, giving me a perfect view of the swells of her breasts.

Dear God. Her tits are exactly where I want to bury my face. All night long.

"That's so incredibly arousing," I rasp out.

"I know," she murmurs. She stands tall again and slides her right hand down her breasts toward her legs, and I go up in flames.

She reaches behind her, unties the apron at her neck, and lets the top fall, revealing . . .

A new bra.

This one is white lace, and it's even better than the last. It suits her. She's a woman made for white lace.

I lick my lips. I want to be smothered in the lust I'm feeling for her.

She unties the apron at the waist and tosses it at me.

I catch it, laughing, grateful for the momentary relief from the gallons of sexual tension flooding my body and brain.

"Nice catch," she says.

"I still have some baseball skills."

"Maybe next time you can show off your other skills. Do a fireman thing. Like a fireman stripper."

"That can be arranged," I say as she pivots, giving me a fantastic view once again of her ass, half of her cheeks exposed in her white panties.

She takes a step, looks back at me, then loses her footing. My hands shoot out, and I reach for her as she stumbles into my lap.

The music still plays, but it's as if the house has gone silent. The quiet enrobes us, wrapping us in decision time.

My hands are cinched on her hips.

I don't say anything.

She doesn't either.

Instead, she inches closer, scooting nearer to me.

A cue.

I let go of her hips, lift my hands to her hair, and unclip it, letting it fall in gorgeous blonde strands down her back. She gasps.

I move her hair to the side and press a soft kiss to her neck. A groan works its way up my throat. "Arden?"

"Yes?" That one word is full of so much desperate need.

It's time to let her know that *yes* is what I want from her. That *yes* is how I feel.

"Whatever comes next, I don't want to mime it."

34

ARDEN

I've never thought of myself as a risk-taker. It's not that I'm scared of taking chances. It's that I'm a plotter. When I've made big choices—where to go to college, how to open a business, when to buy a home—I've done all my homework.

I'm a person who likes to prep. Technically, I can say I've prepped for this possibility during the last week.

But I'm most definitely taking a risk.

A huge one.

One my body is positively begging me to take.

As I turn my face toward Gabe, it's not only my body urging me on. It's my heart. It thumps loudly against my chest for him. This man has earned it, and I want him to have my heart, my mind, my body.

I don't think he was trying to win me, but the race is nearly run, and I'm pretty sure my heart wants to cozy up with him. He's kind and funny and good, and so damn sexy. He takes care of me, and he pushes me when I need it. He's a friend, but he's so much more, and I want the here and now, and I want the after.

My chest tightens, though, because I don't know if he feels the same.

Even so, I'm going to dive in.

Risk our friendship.

Risk my heart.

Sometimes, desire is stronger than logic.

Hell, maybe it is all the time.

I turn around, straddling him, and I clasp his face in my hands. His eyes glimmer with beautiful desire, with a lust that ignites me from head to toe. How is it possible to be more aroused? But it is, and I am. I'm dying for him. For this man I shouldn't be falling for except that it's too late. I've fallen for him, and I want more than one night.

This might be a mistake, but I'll deal with that in the morning. I can't stand the thought of losing him as a friend, but right now I can't stand the thought of this night ending either.

Everything crackles between us, like the air before a lightning strike. We *are* the lightning strike. He licks his lips, and the need to kiss him is maddening.

I've been building up to this moment, to speaking my mind, to feeling empowered. I am empowered as I tell him exactly what I want. "Let's give in tonight. Because I want to kiss you so much I might go insane."

His lips part on a sexy groan. "Let's give in and go mad together." His hands lace through my hair, and in a second, in the span of a heartbeat, they're curled around my head, and he's pulled me close, his mouth claiming mine.

We kiss.

It's not slow. It's not an exploration. It's a supernova, a burst of light and heat. He claims my mouth, and I claim him right back, kissing ferociously. We are fierce new lovers, taking, giving.

Wanting.

His hands rope through my hair, and I hold his face, my thumbs running over his stubbled jawline as we devour each other's mouths.

Our tongues skate together, our breaths mingle. Excitement blares through me. This is what he promised. This is what I've sought. To be kissed into blissful oblivion. And I want him to know. I want to tell him. Somehow, I extricate myself, my breath coming faster. "Blissful oblivion," I murmur. "That was most definitely blissful oblivion."

"It was. And I've wanted it for so long."

"You have?" My voice rises with wonder. Has he wanted me before this one-week project? I've never considered that. Never thought that was a remote possibility.

He tugs me closer. "So goddamn long. I want you so much. I know you want to be friends, but right now . . . tonight?" He takes a beat, stares into my eyes. "Let me be your lover."

No words have ever thrilled me more. A surge of pleasure races through me, settling between my legs in an insistent hum. I can't think about what he means by *how long* because all I can think is *right now*. "Yes," I moan, and I dive back into the kiss.

This time it's more than a kiss. It's a grind and a press. It's a prelude to fucking.

I rock my pelvis against him, feeling the hard outline of his erection, pressing my breasts against him, seeking contact everywhere.

My thoughts go foggy. They're nothing but a haze of pleasure.

His hands slink around my back, and he unhooks my bra, my breasts falling free. He pulls back, and a hiss falls from his mouth—a hiss of appreciation—as he gazes at me. "Have I mentioned you ought to be worshipped? Do you know how that feels?"

"Show me."

He lowers his mouth to a breast, licking and sucking and driving me out of my mind. He lavishes attention on each one, and I'm keenly aware that my good friend has my boobs in his mouth . . . and yet, it feels so unbelievably right.

So unbelievably good.

Like it's meant to be this way—friendship on fire.

I'm aching everywhere, exquisitely and desperately. Every flick of his tongue, every groan from his lips makes me throb more. *"Gabe."*

He lets go with a hungry sigh and looks at me with sapphire irises full of heat.

I flash back to our night on the rocks by the water. He started then to teach me to dirty talk. I'm a quick study, and he lit the match, kindling the fire already in me.

But there was something I didn't practice saying that night.

Something I've been dying to say.

To him.

I bend closer, brush my lips against his. I'm drunk on desire, I'm high with lust, and most of all, I'm floating on this newfound brazen confidence he helped me discover.

I don't know what to do with the way my heart leaps toward him. He's the man I've fallen for, but I'll have to sort that out tomorrow.

Tonight, he's my lover.

I run my thumb along his jaw. "Fuck me hard."

35

GABE

The woman has spoken. I grab her wrists, lift her off me, and lead her around the piece of furniture. "If memory serves, you wanted to know what it would be like to be taken over the back of the couch."

Her eyes shimmer with anticipation. "You remembered."

I run my fingers down her soft skin, through the valley of her breasts, on a path to her belly button. "I listen to everything you say."

"I think that's why I'm so turned on," she whispers as she reaches for the buttons on my shirt and makes quick work of them, spreading open the fabric. She places her hands over my pecs, and I shudder.

"Fuck, that feels good."

"*You* feel good," she corrects.

"You have no idea how long I've wanted your

hands on me." Apparently, I'm unable to keep these feelings bottled up. I really ought to be more circumspect, but with Arden's fingers traveling over my skin, pushing off the sleeves of my shirt, running down my arms, it's hard to think straight.

All I can do is feel.

And it feels fucking wonderful to be touched by her at last. With eager hands, curious fingers, and that hungry look in her big brown eyes, she seems as lost in tonight as I am. But time is ticking since my shift starts soon. I snap open the top button on my jeans, and her hands dart out to undo my fly.

She practically rips down the zipper, and because I'm a helpful sort of fellow, I remove my boxer briefs in a split second. My cock is all too happy to say hello with a proper salute.

She draws a breath as she stares at me, and I couldn't be happier that she must like what she sees. "Can I touch?"

Laughing, I answer her. "You better."

When she wraps her hand around my dick, my thoughts go haywire, and my blood heats up. I want to record all these sensations as she strokes me, since I've wanted it for so damn long, but I'm too turned on.

I'm nothing but nerve endings, invigorated.

I'm only lust, charging through me.

And more too. I'm consumed with the wish to pleasure her. The need to make her feel so damn good. To show her I adore her. And I'll have to do that with my body, since that's how we're communicating tonight.

But most of all, I want her to know I've been listening all along.

Arden doesn't want me to make slow, sweet love to her in a bed. She doesn't want missionary. She wants to be taken.

I wrap my hand over hers, stopping her. "You need to be naked. Right the fuck now."

She shivers, nodding, an inviting sigh falling from her lips. I slide down her panties, and all the air rushes from my lungs. I drink in her beauty. "You're so fucking pretty."

She smiles shyly, and that does it for me. That's the nice girl still inside this naughty one. There's the sweetness in her I fell for from the start.

Grabbing a condom from my wallet, I set it on the furniture then kick off my shoes and push down my jeans. I cup her jaw. "Now, listen. As much as I want to look at your beautiful face, I know what you want, and it's a good and proper fucking. So turn around, hands on the couch, ass up, so I can fuck you into blissful oblivion."

She follows my orders. Her lush body is bent at the sofa, ready, wet, waiting.

Waiting for my hand. I bring my palm against her cheek, eliciting a mind-bending groan of pleasure from her.

Then I slap the other cheek, and she lifts her ass higher. The view is to die for, but as much as I'd love to spend more time introducing her to an intermediate course on the joys of spanking, I need to be inside her.

Badly.

I roll on the condom and slide the head of my dick through her wetness. "Honey, you're so fucking soaked."

She moans. "I know."

"This is the sexiest thing I've felt," I say, rubbing my dick against all that fantastic slickness.

"It's because I want you," she says, and her voice is dripping with desire.

I sink deep inside her in one luxurious thrust, and once I'm fully seated, I let the pleasure wash over me in waves. Ecstasy grips every cell in my body as my hands travel down her back, stopping at her hips.

I start to move, and we find a rhythm quickly as I anchor myself at her waist, wrapping an arm around her. The angle is damn near perfection, and like this I can slide my hand between her legs, stroking the delicious rise of her clit.

She shudders as I fuck her. As I move my hips at a steady pace. As I sink deeper.

She makes the most enticing sounds the whole time, noises that spur me on. Relentless pleasure pounds in my body as I fuck her harder.

"Does this feel good?" I know she loves to talk. I need to give her every chance.

"Yes. It's so good, so good."

I grunt. "You like the way I fuck you?"

"I love the way you fuck me." Her voice is cracking, and I love it. I fucking love it.

She tightens around me, as she cries out, "I'm coming, oh God, I'm coming."

Glorious music to my ears.

I drive into her, fucking her through her orgasm, and once she comes down, I pull out, gripping the condom. "Couch. Now. Ride me."

A few seconds later, I'm sitting on the couch and she's straddling me again, lowering herself on my cock, and hell, this is even better.

I'm back inside her, and now I can look at her, run a hand through her hair, touch her face. "I want to see you. Want to watch you when I make you come again."

"Do you think I can come again?"

"I have no doubt."

I move her hips up and down, helping her find her pace, seek her pleasure. I yank a handful of her hair, and she groans.

"Get your mouth on mine. Let me kiss you."

She dips her face to me, and our tongues collide, my pulse slamming higher.

We're kissing as we're fucking, but soon it's too hard to keep kissing. Our mouths fall away, and she rides me, meeting my gaze.

For that second, it seems like she might look away because it's too intense, too much. But she doesn't. She stares into my eyes and whispers my name.

"Gabe, it's so good with you."

I swear fireworks go off inside me. In my heart. In my body. "It's so fucking good with us, Arden. With *us*."

I want to tell her more. Tell her why. Tell her it's because I'm so in love with her. But the pleasure rides roughshod over my skin, stealing brain cells, stealing breath.

Soon, she's cresting the hill again, and I'm right there behind her, coming hard inside the woman I want to love like this every night.

* * *

After we clean up, the time on my phone laughs at me. It says I need to get the hell out of here. Good thing I slept during the day, so I can be ready to tackle whatever comes our way tonight at the firehouse.

But I don't want to simply walk out. I want to build on this foundation that's most decidedly not friendship anymore.

After I pull on my clothes and she grabs a skimpy little robe that makes me wish I could stay and rip it off her, I decide to take a chance. I've wanted to ask her out for so long. I've been planning to since last week. Her request derailed my strategy, but only temporarily. It's time to drive this train out of the station.

I clear my throat, square my shoulders, and dive into the deep end. "I had a good time tonight. Did you?"

She laughs then rolls her eyes. "Uh, yeah."

Okay, so we're going with humor, with keeping it light. "What if we tried this again?"

Her eyes widen in surprise, as if I've spoken Portuguese. "This?" She gestures to the living room, the scene of the orgasmic crimes.

"Yes. This, and other things. We could go on a date, I thought. Go out." Isn't it obvious what I'm saying?

Her expression shifts to worry. "I'm not sure . . ."

That's not entirely the answer I was hoping for, or expecting, to be honest. "You're not sure of what? If you want to date? Or something else?"

She nibbles on the corner of her lips. "I'm not sure because what if it doesn't . . ."

She doesn't finish the sentence—*work out*.

As much as I'm dying for a yes tonight, I don't want to pressure her. I brush a soft kiss to her lips, tasting her breath. "Don't answer tonight. Think about it."

"It's all I'll think about."

"Me too."

I leave, because soon enough I'll be at work and

inevitably there will be a call coming in and I won't be able to think about her. But maybe that's for the best.

36

ARDEN

Perri is on traffic duty.

Vanessa is shopping for balls.

New bowling balls, that is.

My friend Finley is holed up inside her little yellow cottage trying to meet a deadline for her TV script.

As for me, I've sold three wine country cookbooks, two copies of *The Wife Between Us*, a handful of Stephen Kings, Frederick Backman's newest, a bunch of journals, and countless *Diary of a Wimpy Kid* hardcovers. That Wimpy Kid never goes out of style. I guess as long as humans keep multiplying, their offspring eventually enter the Wimpy Kid fan club.

But even with the steady stream of customers, I wish my girls were around. I'm tempted to call an emergency lunch to discuss Gabe's do-this-again proposal, but I know they're both busy today, and really, I should sort through it on my own for now.

To have sex and date or not to have sex and date. That is the question.

"Think this is useful?" A bright-eyed, lip-glossed blonde slides a pink hardcover on the counter, on top of another book, a guide to the best drinks for any situation.

I smile. "I think no one should ever order a wine cooler or a Jack and Coke on the first date."

She arches a brow in curiosity. "Is that one of the guidelines?"

"No, but it should be. It's one of my personal mantras."

She lifts a curious brow. "What would you order at a bowling alley?"

"Beer."

"At the new bistro down the street?"

"A Cab, some kind of great, full-bodied red."

"And what if you were stalking your ex?"

Laughing, I answer, "A Moscato. It's delicious at first, then leaves a bad taste in your mouth, so it'll remind you why he's the ex."

She laughs harder and flicks her hair off her shoulders. "You do know you just made it so I don't need to buy this book?"

I shrug. "You should report me to the Committee of Bookstore Owners, then. Let them know I misbehaved."

She laughs harder. "Actually, you just made me want to read this even more. I hope it's as good as the warm-up act."

I nod approvingly, tapping the book. "I've thumbed through this. It's hilarious. You'll enjoy it, and if you don't, come back and exchange it."

"Thanks." After I ring her up, she says, "You know, I'm not going to report you to the Committee of Bookstore Owners. I'd rather tell them that you helped convince me to buy this book. In fact, I'm going to snag another as a gift for my best friend."

"She'll love it too," I say confidently.

The woman laughs, shaking her head. "He's a guy. But he'll like it just the same."

A flush crosses my cheeks. I swallow down my awkward reply as I ring up two books. Of all people, I should have known better. I've bought books for a guy friend. I'd like to keep buying books for him.

When she leaves, Henry saunters by, swishing his tail. "What would you do?" I ask him, since I'm alone.

He lifts his furry chin, parks his rear on the floor, and proceeds to take a bath.

"You're no help."

My first instinct is to tell Gabe about that customer. To share the moment with him. If I'm dating him, can I still do that?

The unmistakable sound of a delivery truck pulling up in front of the store lands on my ears, and a few seconds later, the UPS man pushes open the door, a big box in his arms. "Shipment for you, Ms. East."

"Thanks, Barney."

"Where do you want this? It's a heavy one." He reads the name of the publisher, and my eyes light up.

I nearly jump for joy. "That must be the new Robert Galbraith."

His brow knits. "Sounds fancy."

"It's J. K. Rowling. That's her pen name for mysteries."

"The lady who wrote about the wand choosing the wizard?"

"The one and only."

"I saw the movies."

I die a little inside. "You can set them right here."

After he leaves, I grab my X-Acto blade and slice open the box, squealing with delight to find the new book. It releases early next week. I run a hand reverently over the jacket, reveling in the smooth finish, then gently open the book and draw a deep breath and inhale the scent of paper.

This is better than perfume.

This is my favorite scent.

I sneak a glance at the first page, and chills sweep over me, chased by giddiness. I can't wait to share this with Gabe's mom, to sneak a copy over to her and delight in the look in her eyes when she sees the booty I've plundered for her.

But as quickly as that thought arrives, another one slides in. *Can I do that?*

Sure, if we're dating, I can easily give his mom a gift. But what if it doesn't work out between us?

What if the dates peter away? That's his MO. He dates and moves on, and more power to him. But he hasn't exactly indicated he wants more than sex and a date.

And if our dates fade away, would I still set aside books for him to give her? Would we still be friends in the same way?

Or at all?

That's why I said, *What if it doesn't work out?* I don't want to risk our friendship for a casual string of sex dates. I don't want to risk it unless we're both taking a chance at the biggest of prizes.

My stomach pitches, churning with that abhorrent thought. I try to shake it off. We'd be fine, right? We'd stay friends. It'd be the same—we'd make sure of it. We'd have sex again, and date, and then . . .

I don't know what would happen next, so I focus on the now.

I lug the box to the storeroom in the back, safely stowing the treasures away until I can sell them.

I head to the new fiction shelves and begin arranging the books, when a shelf wobbles the slightest bit—the one Gabe texted me about the other day, asking if it was okay.

It was okay then.

Or so I thought.

I glance around for a cat, in case one of them knocked it looser somehow.

But Henry's moved his hygiene to the window

and is giving his boy parts a very thorough licking for the whole town square to see.

"Get a room," I say to him, then scan for Clare, finding her sprawled out on the floor, napping luxuriously in a ray of sunlight. I fiddle with the shelf again, trying to figure out where it's loose, but I'm not handy. I can cook, I can clean, but I'm not known for my skills with a hammer and a nail.

I turn away from the shelf, heading to the counter to text Gabe.

He's my go-to guy, after all.

But I stop when I open his contact.

How will he be my go-to guy if we take the chance of dating? Or, more so, how will he be my go-to guy *after*?

Because, I gulp, remembering his words.

I had a good time tonight. What if we tried this again? This, and other things. We could go on a date.

He asked me to date. But he asked me to screw again too.

For all I know, that's how he asked out Darla, and look where she is. She's not hanging in the friend zone. She's in the cold zone.

Fact is, I like the friend zone. The friend zone is safe. I don't want to be unfriended, and that's a distinct possibility if our dating goes haywire.

He only said he wants to do it again. He didn't say he wanted to be mine. I didn't speak my truth either, yet now as I look at last night in the clear light of day, I don't think there was a reason to put myself on the line like that. To let him know I want much more than sex and dates.

There wasn't, because he didn't say he wanted to go all in.

He only wants to go all in with sex.

And I want it all.

That's when I realize I'm in this way too deep.

The only way to save myself, to save the friendship, is to stay friends.

I find the hammer in my office and fix the shelf myself, but it's still a little loose, and that leaves me with a tight, cold knot in my throat.

37

GABE

Let the record reflect that I'm not happy that anyone suffered an asthma attack, was struck by a vehicle, or experienced a mild seizure.

I *am* thrilled none of the incidents resulted in serious injuries.

Selfishly, I'm also glad that all of them, as well as the brush fire on a hillside by the highway that we extinguished in twenty-five minutes, kept my mind off Arden.

There's no room for thinking about women when you have to put out flames.

But now my shift is ticking near to closing time. As Shaw and I check the equipment on the truck, he gestures toward Charlie, who's hanging out with us at the end of his shift. One of his last shifts. "Did you hear Charlie's boss says he found a new guy already?"

"That so?"

Charlie affects a frown. "They don't let the bodies get cold in our field."

"He's not starting for another week or so, but yeah, the boss man found someone from . . ." Shaw stops and scratches his head. "Hell, he told me when I saw him at the ER, and I already forgot."

I'm tempted to make a wisecrack about his mind going to hell, like I usually do, but I'm not in the mood to joke.

Which is odd, since I usually am.

But I'm antsy, waiting to hear from Arden. As we wrap up the checklist, my phone dings with a text from her.

Arden: Working late. Doing inventory. Are you almost done?

Smiling, I figure she must want to see me ASAP.

It's ten, and it's been quiet for a spell. Plus, her store is only two blocks away. I clap Shaw on the back. "I'm going to see Arden for a few minutes. Call me if anything comes up, okay?"

His eyes widen in surprise. "A booty call? You dog."

I roll my eyes. "Yes, exactly. I'm going to her

store for a quickie in the stacks. No, you dickhead. But I did finally tell her how I felt."

"About time. And what did the future Mrs. Harrison say?"

"That's what I'm going to go and find out." I rub my hands together, a burst of excitement zipping through me.

"Get the hell out of here, Casanova."

A few minutes later, I knock on the door to A New Chapter. It's dark inside. Only a few lights flicker. She walks to the door, looking as gorgeous as she did when I left her last night. Maybe more. She opens the door, and I half expect a kiss.

Wait.

I wholly expect a kiss.

Instead, she smiles faintly, the kind that doesn't quite reach her eyes. "Thanks for coming."

And no kiss is coming my way. Judging from her serious expression, I'm not getting the yes I was hoping for either.

My shoulders slump, but I keep my tone light. "No problem."

"I thought about what you said."

I grit my teeth, trying to swallow my own pending disappointment as I wait for her to speak again.

"I value our friendship too much. I don't want to lose you, Gabe."

"I don't want to lose you either."

"And today, I was thinking about all these things. Giving books to your mom, and telling you stories about my day, and hearing your stories, and visiting your pops, and rescuing Hedwig, and going bowling. I don't know how we can do that. Because what if it doesn't work out?"

"But . . ." I start, thinking of all the ways I can convince her it'll work out.

Except maybe she doesn't want to be convinced. Maybe she wants an out, and a gracious one. An escape hatch that'll preserve what matters most—the foundation we've built of friendship.

And if she wants an out, I suppose this is the lesser of two evils—her letting me down now before we try to become something more, instead of her letting me down when I'm in even deeper.

I drum my fingers against the shelf, a little loose. "Hey, no worries. I hear ya. I get it." I study the wood, grateful for the distraction. "Want me to fix this?"

"You don't have to."

I wave a hand, making it clear this is no big deal. "Nah, it's easy. I know where you keep the tools."

I head to her office, grab the tool set, and fix the shelf in two minutes. I want to show her I do understand. I do respect her boundaries. I don't want her to think I'm going to vault past them simply because she shared some secrets with me about her sexual fantasies. Besides, she made her intentions clear from the start. Maybe we both crossed a line last night, but that happens in the heat of the moment, sort of like when two actors fall for each other on set. We were playacting, stage fighting, and stage fucking.

When the curtain falls, the romance ends.

I try to rattle the shelf, pleased it won't budge. I pronounce it good as new.

"Gabe," she says, like my name pains her. "I'm sorry."

She's not talking about the shelf. But a knife's nicking away at my heart, and it's hard to pretend it doesn't hurt as I stare at the person wielding the blade. I do my best when I answer her. "Fixing it was easy."

"I meant about—"

I slice that notion off at the knees. "Hey, we're good." I tuck my finger under her chin. "Never ever worry about us. We are all good. I promise."

"You swear?" Her voice trembles.

I lie. "I do." I pile onto the lie. "In fact, let's go bowling on Saturday. Like we always do. Your week of studies is nearly over. I'd say you passed with flying colors, learned all you needed, and we can get back to seven-letter words that lead to pizza being on you."

"Or maybe I'll kick your butt," she says, and she sounds like she's faking it too.

Maybe we'll both fake it for a little while, but for different reasons, until we return to our balance.

I return the tools to her office, and when I leave,

a call comes in for a small restaurant fire. Battling the blaze takes my mind momentarily off the way my heart seems charred to a crisp by a word I once thought was wonderful.

Friend.

38

ARDEN

I stare at the dessert I made the other night.

The uneaten dessert.

Like a zombie, on Friday morning I trudge toward the plate of coconut bars tucked in the corner of my kitchen counter. I pick up one, studying it like a scientist, holding it to the kitchen light, considering it from this angle, that angle.

We didn't touch any of these. They've been here since two nights ago when we made love.

"Ugh."

I mean . . . when we fucked.

When he took me over the back of my couch like I wanted.

When he gave me a fantasy from my list.

That's all it was.

That's all I can believe it was, yet my spine shivers from the memory.

"Stop it, body. Just stop it."

But I replay the scene again, picturing the moment when he hooked his arm around my waist, then when he went so deep I saw stars.

And the sensation returns. Intensifies. Builds like a storm inside me.

"You are a traitorous bitch," I say to my lower half. "One taste of him and you're hungry for more."

I bite into a hunk of the coconut bar, chewing as I head to the back door, stepping onto the porch. The morning sun blinds me, like it's fair that the sky is so perfectly clear, like it's fair that the day is so deliciously warm.

After last night, the sky should be punishing me with pelting cold rain.

Last night was a punch to the ribs—of my own doing, but nonetheless, that's what it was. My muscles ache, my head hurts, and my throat feels raw.

I take another bite of the bar, but the coconut is cardboard to me. Telling Gabe I only wanted to be friends tasted like the worst lie in the world. I don't want to be friends. I want to be *everything*.

I sink onto the steps, sadness shrouding me, my heart caving. A robin swoops down, hopping across the grass.

I remember the robins and their hunt for cheese and crackers the day David dumped me at Silver Phoenix Lake. That same fateful day my friendship with Gabe launched.

I toss the remains of the coconut bar to the bird. Chirping, he pecks at it, and I try to laugh, to tell myself this is funny and I'll share the story with Gabe. But it's not any easier to return to our normal today than it was yesterday. The prospect of starting a Words with Friends game with him makes my head throb.

I pick myself up, shower, and change my clothes.

I can't wallow all day. I'm a doer. So, I *do*. Grabbing the book I brought home last night, I head to my car and drive over to Gabe's mom's house. When she answers, I flash a smile. "Hi, Mrs. Harrison."

"Hey, Arden, good to see you. Want to come in? Gabe's not here."

"That's okay. I was looking for you anyway."

"You were?"

I lean in close, whispering conspiratorially, "Don't tell the Bookstore Police."

Her blue eyes sparkle, just like his. "Oh! More top secret goodies."

I hand her the Robert Galbraith, adding my best *everything is fine* smile. "Just for you."

She clutches the treasure to her chest. "I'm diving in today." Then she wraps her arms around me. "You're such a wonderful friend to my son. What would I do without you?"

Her words are my reminder. This is why I did what I did. To preserve what we've had.

Our friendship is a gift, and I treasure it the same way I do words and stories.

As I walk away, I tell myself giving up the chance for more has to be worth it.

39

GABE

Some things stay the same.

The day after she turns me down, I run. I cut across town, tuning into a *Surprise Me* playlist on Google Play.

I make a path past the springs, toward the hill, and right to Silver Phoenix Lake as a song from the Heartbreakers comes on.

"About a Girl."

Some tune about how men will change their lives for a girl.

I shake my head. "No shit."

The line about falling hard and changing everything is a slap in the face.

"I did fall hard," I mutter. "I wanted to change everything."

I run up the trail, running past the spot where I found Arden more than a year ago, flashing back to that fateful day.

I should have known then I'd wind up right where I am—with an aching in my chest. I should have known because whatever feelings I'd already had for her—the crush that kicked in the first time I met her—didn't vacate when I saw snot running down her nose. When I witnessed her tears for another man. The way I felt for her only intensified.

She was crying in her crackers then, and I still found her endearing.

Kind.

Clever.

And beautiful.

After eight punishing miles of trying to drain my thoughts of her, I do what I did that day. I run to my parents' house. As I turn the corner to their block, a red car fades in the distance, cruising the other way.

Her car?

Hell, that's a crazy thought.

Must be another red car.

When I go inside, my mom waves from the couch. "Do not disturb. I'm reading the new Robert Galbraith."

"Isn't that out on—?"

Before I say *Tuesday*, I know Arden was here, stopping by to give my mom a gift. My chest hollows, a big gaping hole that I wish I could fill with how I feel for her. If she keeps being herself, she's going to make it awfully hard to get over her.

I head to the kitchen, and when my dad offers me a coffee, he asks what's going on with her.

"Nothing. That's the trouble. She only wants to be friends."

He pats me on the back. "Sometimes you win, sometimes you lose. Sometimes the girl you want doesn't feel the same."

That's the whole sad, sorry truth.

40

ARDEN

"I'm looking for a book."

I turn away from the shelf of travel guides to a thin man wearing a straw hat.

"Anything in particular?" I try my best to feign cheeriness on Saturday morning. I'm the *happy, happy* bookstore owner today and every goddamn day, even though there's an organ in my chest moping over a guy I can't have.

The man in the hat strokes his goatee. "Can't remember the name. It's about a fireman who has special powers..."

He talks more about the story, but I latch onto one word, thinking of a certain fireman and all his special powers. His charm, his heart, his funny bone. He has so many more powers though. The power to make me feel like I'm special. Like I'm wonderful.

"Do you know it?"

I blink, trying to root myself in the present. "I . . ."

I can't place the book he's talking about.

A voice cuts in. A chipper, confident one. "You mean Joe Hill's *The Fireman*. Yes, we have it in stock," Madeline says, tipping her head to that section and guiding the customer there. She easily locates the novel and rings him up.

When he's gone, she turns to me. "Are you okay?"

"Just a little off today."

"Go take a walk or something. You're not yourself."

"Maybe I just need to clear my head."

"Take a break for a few. I have this covered."

I turn to go and step outside when I see Mr. Businessman heading in my direction.

I freeze.

He's the reason I went to Gabe in the first place. Is he coming back to try to ask me on a date again? What do I say?

I'm not sure I'll handle it any better this time around, even though the smile on his face expands as he walks toward me.

41

GABE

Another rep. And another. On the weight bench, I make it through more reps than usual.

"Damn, are you hitting the juice?" Shaw asks as we go through our morning workout.

"Yeah, just like I did back in Texas."

"Ah, I always suspected you were a 'roid head in your playing days."

"That's me." My voice is pure monotone.

"How did it go with your lady the other night? Didn't get to ask."

I finish my set, sit up, and scratch my jaw. "Let's see. On a scale of one to ten, it was a negative fifty."

"Ouch. That bad?" Shaw switches to the bench, and I move behind, spotting him.

"She gave me my official *let's be friends forever* card."

"Damn. And you told her how you felt?" He pushes up the weights. "You told her everything?"

I shrug, keeping my hands near the bar. "Pretty sure."

"Pretty sure?"

"I asked her to go out. That's clear, isn't it? Like on a date?"

His eyes widen as he raises the weights again, wincing, then lowering. "And you told her you've had it bad for her for a year?"

"I told her I've wanted her for a long time."

"Wanted?"

"Yes. *Wanted*."

He grunts, lifting. "Dude. She probably feels like a piece of meat."

More like the other way around. "I think I was pretty clear."

"You're *pretty sure* you were 'pretty clear'?" He finishes his set and sits up. "As in, you said you're in love with her?"

"Hell no," I answer defensively.

He furrows his brow like he's deep in thought. "Did you, by any chance, say you were crazy for her?"

"No way." But now he has me wondering if I totally botched my plans to lay it on the line.

He taps his chin. "Wait. Wait. Did you say, 'I have no brains'?"

I sigh heavily. "All right. Spit it out. What should I have said?"

He doesn't answer because a dark-haired guy with a swirl of sunburst tats up his left arm strides over to us. "Hey there. Any chance one of you can spot me? I'd appreciate it."

"Go for it." Shaw moves behind him, and the guy starts lifting, using more weights than either of us. "Damn. You training hard for a fight, bro?"

The guy laughs, barely breaking a sweat as he lifts. "Nah, my fighting days are behind me. I'm turning over a new leaf as a pacifist."

Shaw arches a brow. "For real?"

"I'm kidding. Well, I'm all for world peace. But no, I just need to stay in shape for work. I'm starting a new job in a few days."

"Lifting heavy shit?"

"*Bodies. Very heavy bodies sometimes,*" he says, playing up the spooky card, as he raises the bar. Then, he's pure deadpan as he answers. "I'm a paramedic. And sometimes the bodies are quite heavy."

I look at Shaw knowingly then say, "Welcome to the club. Well, we're at the local firehouse, so we'll be seeing you around."

"No shit?" He sets down the bar, wipes his palms against each other, and offers a hand to shake. "Good to meet you. I'm Derek McBride. Just moved here from San Francisco. Some other guy is heading back home, right?"

Shaw answers, "Yeah, that's Charlie. Friend of ours."

"Sorry to hear he had to go, then. It's never fun when a good bud moves away."

"So are we," I say, then make the official intros to Shaw and myself. "But let us know if you need anything. Rescue workers—we look out for each other, right?" I knock fists with Shaw, then the new guy.

"Amen to that." Derek scratches his jaw. "Speaking of, I've been looking for a place to stay. It's getting crowded as hell where I am right now. Couches are the worst."

"The absolute worst," Shaw echoes.

"And finding a decent rental in this town is harder than tracking down a beer for less than $5. Do you happen to know anyone in town who has a place to rent?"

Shaw grins. "As a matter of fact, I do. I'll hook you up. And you'll find cheap beers at The Barking Pug. Awesome dive bar off the main drag."

"Dive bars are the best kind."

Shaw grabs me by the shoulders, then speaks to Derek in a deliberately leading-the-witness voice. "Also, don't you think Gabe should tell the woman he loves how he truly feels about her?"

Derek grins. "Always. Always let the woman know how you feel."

He gives a quick wave then takes off.

When we finish working out, Shaw punches my shoulder. "And you, dipshit, think about what I said. Think about whether you said all you needed to say to her."

As if I can think about anything else.

As I head home, I replay that last night at her house.

My questions.

What if we tried to be more than friends? To date. Go out.

At the time, my meaning seemed patently clear. But now, with a few days' perspective, was it?

I flash back to my year in the majors, and it feels like déjà vu. Was I simply warming up in the bull pen with Arden? Rather than going full tilt in a game with a pennant on the line?

More importantly, what if Shaw is right?

Later, I head over to see the one person who tells it like it is. I'll never sort it out for myself, and I can't let this uncertainty go on a moment longer.

42

ARDEN

Empirically, he's good-looking.

But as the handsome man strides toward me, all I can think about is the man I want to be playing Fifty Shades of Everything with.

Not this guy. And if he asks me out again, I'll turn him down like a big girl this time. Using my words.

Only . . .

He doesn't look at me. He's looking elsewhere. He breezes right past me. Like he doesn't even see me.

He says, "Hello," and then the next words out of his mouth shock me. "You must be Darla."

What the what?

I whip around as Mr. Businessman meets Darla in front of the coffee shop next to A New Chapter. Darla takes his hand and shakes it.

"So great to meet you. I'm Hank," he says.

"Vince told me you were pretty, but you're even prettier in person."

Who the heck is Vince?

She laughs, a pretty tinkling sound. "And you're a perfect gentleman, but that's exactly what my cousin told me."

Okay, this Vince fellow is Darla's cousin, and he must have set them up on a blind date.

"He's a good friend. Plus, I paid him. No, just kidding." Hank the businessman hooks his thumb first toward the coffee shop then down the street. "I like coffee, but there's a great ice cream shop around the corner that has birthday cake and blueberry ice cream this month. Any chance you want to go there instead?"

"Let's blow this popsicle stand."

I slink against the wall like I can blend into it, but they're only looking at each other as Hank, the man who wanted to date me, and Darla, the woman who dated Gabe, head to an ice cream shop to eat my favorite flavor.

They're living their lives. Enjoying themselves together as they get to know each other. This feels like karma, only I'm not sure what to make of it. Is this a sign that I need to live my life? But which version of it?

I shake my head, trying to understand why I feel anything about these two people I hardly know.

Especially jealousy.

I'm a little jealous they're dating.

That they've moved on. That they're enjoying the next thing in their lives, having ice cream for lunch on a Saturday.

I go for a walk through the town square, calling Finley and telling her about the blind date I just witnessed, since she loves to hear romance tales that might inspire a TV episode.

"Ice cream dates have traditionally been known to lead to happily ever afters," she remarks in her usual wry and chipper tone.

I try to laugh, but it sounds as empty as I feel. "I would like an ice cream date," I say, a little sad. A lot sad.

"So go get one."

But really what I want is the happily part. And the ever. And the after.

"That's the thing. I'm not sure how to do that."

She hums, like she's thinking. "But maybe you do actually know."

Do I though?

I say goodbye, then wander along the side streets, reflecting, thinking, till I wind up on a block where Perri's been running traffic duty. I find her talking to a well-built guy with a left arm covered in ink. He's straddling a motorcycle, his helmet in his hand.

She stares sharply at him. "I'm going to let you off with a warning this time. But do us all a favor and obey the law. Can you do that?"

He winks at her. "Anything for you."

She points at the pavement. "Hit the road, mister. Before I decide to stop being the nice cop and write you a ticket instead."

"Maybe I'll see you around, *nice cop*."

"Maybe you'll be better off if you don't."

"A man can dream." He takes off, the bike rumbling in his wake.

I close the distance to her. "Who's that?"

"Someone who's too hot for his own good."

"Or for your good?"

"Ha. I'm immune to hot, inked men on bikes."

"Right." We both know there's no vaccine for her on that count.

"What's his name?"

"Derek McBride."

"Hot name."

"Hot name for a hot guy, but nothing will come of it." She tilts her head, looks me over. "You okay?"

I heave a sigh. "I've been better."

She rubs my shoulder briefly. "What's wrong?"

I draw a breath, and my heart shakes. My voice wobbles. If I speak, I might cry. But I do it anyway, blurting out, "I'm in love with Gabe."

She smiles sympathetically. "Oh, honey, I know." She wraps me in a hug, petting my hair. "What are we going to do about it?"

I sniffle. "I don't know. He doesn't feel the same way."

She jerks back, staring at me. "Are you sure? You told us what happened after you had sex, but do you really think he's not in love with you too?"

I shrug, as a tear slinks down my cheek.

"Arden, you're a smart girl, and I'd encourage you to review the signs."

"Which ones?" I choke out. "The one where he said *let's do this again*?"

"No. The last year of your life."

The last year.

I let it flash before me, from the day on the trail, to when I brought treats to the firehouse a week later, to our first game of Words with Friends. I move on to other memories, from how he makes sure we spend time together, to his asking me to meet his pops, to the way he touched me in the elevator the other day. He even invited me to dinner with his parents. My God, he wants me to spend time with his family.

Most of all, I linger on the way he looked at me when I opened the door in burgundy lace.

Like he wanted me desperately.

But it was more than physical, wasn't it?

I recall the fire in his eyes, how there was so much more than lust. He gazed at me like he wanted . . .

Do I dare to let myself believe this?

But it feels completely true.

He looked at me like he wanted all of me.

Like he wanted me the same way I want him.

I want him in all the ways.

And maybe, just maybe, he didn't say it. After all, I didn't speak my truth. I didn't bare my soul for him and tell him he's become my everything. Hell, I said, *What if it doesn't work out?* I didn't even answer him. Maybe neither one of us said all that needed to be said.

Because our friendship isn't worth risking for a few more fucks.

It is worth risking for something bigger. For something that might be everything.

My belief that I could keep him in the friends-only lane was foolish. Gabe Harrison infiltrated the romance zone as soon as we started our project, truth be told. Once we picked up Hedwig then talked about our turn-ons in the Garden of Eden, I felt that tug on both body and heart.

The pull only intensified, growing stronger the closer we became. Our sex-ploration made me fall for the man that had been right in front of me all along.

As I replay all the signs I missed, I do what I do best.

I plot. I plan.

I need to find a way to turn this new awareness into a best-laid plan.

43

GABE

I heat up water for tea. "Remember that woman who came by the other day?"

My pops laughs. "The one you're in love with?"

Yeah, he's all here today.

"That's the one." I pour the hot water into a mug with a tea bag.

He winks. "She's a pretty lady. And she has it bad for you too."

"Does she?"

He nods sagely. "It's not as if everything gets past me. Sure, some things do. But love? Little glances? I was a sly fox myself once, and I didn't win Emily over by being obtuse about women."

Laughing, I ask, "How did you win her over?"

He tuts, shaking his head. "Young people." He motions for me to come closer.

I leave the mug on his kitchen counter to steep and join him on the couch.

"Closer."

I scoot over, waiting to receive his wisdom.

He clasps a hand on my shoulder. "Put your heart on the line, young man."

"But how? How should I do it?"

He huffs like he can't quite believe whippersnappers today. "Just tell her you love her. That's all you can do. If she's going to toss you to the wind, she'll toss you, but if you haven't been clear, *be clear*. Back in my day, we didn't futz around the way your generation does. When I knew I loved Emily, it was plain and simple. I spelled it out."

And that's when I know what to do.

But holy hell, it takes fucking forever.

44

ARDEN

"Just wear this. I bought it the other day." Vanessa thrusts a Happy Days bag at me.

"You are an addict. You caved on the mint-green typewriter dress?"

She shakes her head. "Look inside. It's for you."

We're at my house on Saturday night, getting ready. Because you can't really prep to tell a man how you feel without your best girls by your side to help.

I peer into the bag, and my eyes pop. "No, you didn't!"

"Yes, I did."

"You are too much." I brandish the simple periwinkle-blue skirt I checked out the other day, the one with cartoonish images of books on the fabric.

It's short, and it's me, and it's not me trying to ape Vanessa's style. I kick off my capri jeans and slide into the skirt, then find a simple white tank in my bureau and pull it on. I check out my reflection as Perri raises a glass of Chablis.

"Chablis. For when your best friend finally decides she's going to go after her man."

"I am most definitely going after my man," I declare to myself and to my friends.

My man.

That's what I want Gabe to be.

Excitement flares inside me, chased by nerves.

There are no guarantees. I don't have a promise. We won't have a written edict that we'll remain friends. Nor do I know if his heart is banging as wildly for me as mine is for him.

But I'll never know the answer until I try.

There's no substitute for experience.

Some things in life you can't charade your way through. You need to put your neck out.

If he says no, if I'm wrong about how he feels, then I'll turn to my backup plan. To let him know he's stuck with me as a friend. That even if he says *see you later* to a romance, I'm committed to staying friends with him, just like I was committed to thanking him that day a year ago when I brought him treats to the fire station. The man has seen me at my worst, and we became buddies. If we need to do it again, we'll do it again.

But God, I hope he picks Plan A.

I turn around, showing them the outfit. "Does it meet your approval?"

Vanessa cheers. "It's so cute."

Perri points her glass at me. "You look fantastic."

"I'm ready to go take a chance." I toss a glance at Perri. "Speaking of chances, did you tell Vanessa about the guy you busted?"

Vanessa flicks out her tongue salaciously. "She did, and he sounded delish."

Perri leans back on my bed and laughs. "That man had trouble written all over him."

"And you like trouble," Vanessa points out. "You were always the daring one."

"Girls." Perri rises from the bed, lifting her glass. "We are all the daring ones. Now it's Arden's turn to go be daring."

I take a deep breath, drawing in their strength, feeling it mingle with my own confidence. I've always believed in myself. I've never been an insecure girl. But the last week with Gabe has taught me there's no replacement for speaking my mind.

I head to Pin-Up Lanes to meet him for a friendly night of bowling, picking our regular lane, setting up our bowling names on the scoreboard, and then hoping. Hoping that when I go for a strike, I won't strike out.

Once Gabe walks in, my breath catches.

It's not because he's so damn handsome.

It's not because of that confident walk or that easy grin.

It's because tonight marks the first time I've looked at him and let myself *own* my feelings. The first time I've watched him come toward me and known in my heart what I feel is love.

45

ARDEN

When he reaches me, I see he's clutching his phone like it's a lifeline.

"Hey, Arden."

"Hey, Gabe," I say, my brow knitting over the way he's attached to the mobile device.

"You look"—he stares at me up and down, like he did at my house—"beautiful."

I wasn't seeking confirmation, but I love the compliment nonetheless. "You look more handsome than ever. And there's something I want to ask you."

"Okay?" His tone is tentative.

"Do you remember that time I asked for your help with my project, and I made a list?"

He laughs lightly, more sure this time. "You think I've forgotten?"

"No, but it was a week ago. Since then, I've made another list. Because I'm a plotter."

He nods, moving closer. "You're definitely a planner."

"There are new things I want to try, so I wrote them out."

"New things?" His voice is laced with curiosity.

"Yes." Nerves flutter inside me as I take my list from my purse. "Can I read it to you?"

"I'd love to hear it."

I flip open the paper, clear my throat, and dive into the great unknown, clutching fervently to the wish that he might feel the same. "Things I Want to Try."

I meet his blue-eyed gaze, seeing possibility in them. *Here goes the first one.* "One: Being your friend and also your lover."

His eyebrows lift in excitement.

"Two: Doing it outside."

His eyes sparkle.

"Three: Spending the night with you."

The irises dance now with a happiness that matches what's in my heart. It spurs me on.

"Four: Going on dates with you, and only you."

Yes, he mouths.

I love that he can't wait till I'm done to give an answer, but I have more to say so I keep going, the look in his eyes helping me drive it home. "Five: Taking the chance to be with you . . . because I believe you and I are worth it. Do you know why?"

He smiles so wide it's like it reaches another county. I'm about to give the answer to my own question when he cuts in, holding up his phone screen.

I peer at it, reading the three little words he made on the game board. In an instant, joy radiates through me, stretching into every corner of my body. He's spelled I LOVE YOU. "You made a Words with Friends for me?"

He nods, proudly.

"How did you do this?"

"Well, I can't play it, of course, but it took me only, say, 218 games against myself till I came up with one of the letters on the board I needed, and then the rest of the seven letters to play it."

"You were determined," I say with wonder as I read his phone again, my eyes filling with tears of happiness, my heart flooding with love, a love I didn't expect but can't imagine living without.

Now, as I look back on the last year, and the last week especially, I can see this is where our story was heading. Love was always what was written on our pages. I just had to keep reading the book.

"I was determined, and I am determined, because you're worth it." He lets go of the phone and reaches for me, lifting me in his arms. "I love you, Arden East. I love you so damn much."

He drops a kiss to my lips before I can get a word in edgewise, but I don't care, because I'm on a hot air balloon soaring to the stratosphere with him —my friend, my lover, and my man.

"I'm so in love with you. That's what I was going to tell you," I say when we separate.

He presses another soft kiss to my lips, and this is even better than sex. Tingles radiate all through my bones. I sigh happily, savoring every second, delighting in this true and honest kiss that feels like a promise.

But words matter too, so when we stop, I press my hands to his chest. "I don't want to lose you, Gabe. I meant everything I said before. You mean so much to me. I hate the thought of you not being in my life."

He threads a hand through my hair. "Wouldn't you know? Turns out I hate that thought too. So let's stay in each other's lives."

I smile like a woman in love.

And love feels so . . . *empowering*.

So does something else. Another choice I make. I clasp his face, loving the freedom to touch him like this. "What do you say we skip bowling, go to my place or yours, and spend the night together?"

"I'd say I'm game for that. I only have one condition."

"What is it?"

"Tonight, I'm making love to you."

* * *

At my house, he makes good on his promise. He spreads me out on my bed, strips me naked, and worships me with his lips and his tongue. He lavishes my body with kisses, settling between my legs and bringing me to ecstasy. Then he climbs over me, reaching for his wallet.

I stop him, circling my hand around his arm. "I'm on the pill. I want to feel all of you."

He groans his appreciation for that answer, tossing his wallet behind him. It hits the floor with a *thunk*, and he wiggles an eyebrow. "Who cares about the damn wallet right now?"

"Definitely not me."

He spreads my thighs wide, slides inside me, and I wrap my legs around his waist, hooking my ankles together, drawing him closer.

"Arden," he groans, "I've been falling in love with you for a long time."

"Keep falling in love with me," I whisper as he moves luxuriously inside me. "And I'll keep falling in love with you."

He reaches for my wrists, raises them above my head, and pins them, driving me wild, making me love missionary in a whole new way because the man I love is taking me and fucking me and loving me.

The next morning when we wake, I wear nothing but an apron as I pluck eggs from the carton, prepping to cook him breakfast.

Before I can turn on the burner, though, he's found other things to do with my apron. In a flash, I'm on the counter, my wrists tied with the apron strings as he introduces me to new uses for the kitchen, and after that we christen the yard too.

Eventually, a whole lot later, I cook him eggs, and he devours them. After all, he worked up quite an appetite.

I work up an appetite of another kind a few days later when he gives me a striptease. We're talking the full regalia. Fireman suspenders, turnout gear, and a hot-as-hell dance.

Let's just say I give him his reward.

On my knees.

46

ARDEN

A couple of days later, Perri pops by the bookstore and asks if I'm free to grab a bite to eat. I'm finished up, and Madeline is working for the evening, so we head to Helen's Diner, one of our favorite places in town.

"How's love? Is it as fabulous as everyone makes it out to be?" she asks as we sit.

I smile. I can't help it. "It's the most fabulous thing. I highly recommend unexpectedly falling in love with your best guy friend after he gives you hypothetical lessons in seduction that turn real."

She wiggles an eyebrow and taps her temple. "And I'll just file that away under possibilities I never expected."

"Same here. But seriously, Gabe is great, and I'm the luckiest girl in Lucky Falls."

"It's not luck. You went after your happily ever after and you got it.

"And I'm not going to let it go."

"You better not."

Then it's my turn to wiggle my eyebrows, because I want the dish on the guy Perri's been hot for. She thought nothing would come of the man she pulled over, but Derek McBride turned up in her life again in a most unexpected way, and I'm dying for more details. "Tell me all the details about the hottie."

"Whomever would you be referring to?" She plays it coy.

I shoot her a look. "The one you pulled over the other day who looked at you like he wanted to eat you up, toss you over his shoulder, and then pleasure you all night long. That one."

Her eyes twinkle. "He did look at me like that, didn't he?"

"Um, yeah. And if memory serves, I feel like you were giving him the same look."

"You did hit the nail on the head when you said I had a type, and he is definitely it," she says with a laugh as the server comes over to take our order. I opt for a chicken sandwich, and Perri chooses a salad. I steer us back to the conversation. "So, Miss Has a Type and He's It—what's next with him? You ran into him again, you flirted, you had an epic kiss, and now? Tell me what's next?" I'm dying to know.

She sighs, and it seems full of import. "Seems he showed up last night on my doorstep, with his duffel, since my brother went ahead and rented the room above the garage to him."

My eyes bulge. My jaw drops. My head spins. That's a twist I didn't see coming. "That means you're living with the guy you want to bang?"

"Seems the hot guy that I want to bang is now my new housemate."

"That's a bit of a conundrum. You definitely can't bang him if you're living with him."

She tightens her ponytail. "Yes, that would seem to be the wise plan. This landlord shall not bang her housemate."

"The housemate she's oh so tempted by," I add, then I smile. "I can't wait to hear how the non-banging plan unfolds."

EPILOGUE

Gabe

Several months later

"Do I look handsome or do I look handsome?" I hold my hands out wide for my pops as we stroll slowly around the grounds, wandering past gardens of daisies and tulips.

He narrows his eyes, giving me the once-over, appraising the pressed shirt and slacks. "You got your good looks from . . ."

I wait for him to say from him or from Emily or from my mom. But instead, he smiles. "You got your good looks from here." He taps my heart. "It's what's inside that matters."

I smile at him. "Thanks, Pops. But I got my

charm from you."

"No doubt about that. Also, you look handsome as hell, so get out of here and get your girl."

I walk him back to his suite and make sure he's settled in with one of his Dashiell Hammett paperbacks, courtesy of Arden. He parks his reading glasses on his nose, opens the book, then glances up at me. "You make sure Emily sees how handsome you look on your way out. She'd appreciate it."

I don't correct him this time. I let him enjoy this moment when he's slipped back in time. "She would, Pops. She would. Love you."

"Love you too, kiddo."

When I arrive at A New Chapter and peer through the edge of the window, Arden's book club is in full swing. She's expanded her offerings in the last several months, and the Bawdy Ladies—as they've dubbed themselves—have become regulars, spending one night a week discussing books here, along with many other topics.

They've fully enlisted Arden in their crew now, and tonight she's running the club.

But I've enlisted them as well.

If there's one thing I know about Arden, it's that she both loves and leans on the people in her life, from her best friends, to her employee, to these ladies, who've become a regular fixture.

As I scan the premises from my lookout point, I note that Miriam has arranged the circle of chairs as requested. Arden's back is to the door, her hair spilling down her shirt in a beautiful cascade of blonde. I check the time on my watch.

Miriam glances at the door, and I move into her line of sight, nodding that all systems are a go.

Miriam returns her focus to the group, and Madeline, next in line for the plan, opens the door for me.

She flashes me a conspiratorial smile, and I smile in return, moving quietly among the shelves to the back area of the store. Ducking behind the self-help section, I listen to the women as they discuss Liane Moriarty's *Big Little Lies*.

"I suppose what this book made me think about most," Miriam puts in, "is what it really takes to make a marriage work. What do you think, Sara?"

The woman with red cat-eye glasses chimes in. "It takes a whole lot of determination, but kindness and humor too."

Another voice pipes up. CarolAnn, I think. "A good union requires a woman who understands her man, and a man who understands his woman."

That's my cue.

I step around from the shelf. "And it takes a friendship that turned into a great love story."

Arden startles then snaps her gaze to me. "Hey, you." Her voice is soft, curious.

God, I love her so much. I walk to her, meet her gorgeous gaze, then continue. "It takes knowing the other person. Listening to the other person. Giving her space when she needs it and giving her closeness when she craves that. It takes laughter and nights out and nights in, and being willing to look out for what matters to the other person. Personally, I believe it's best when you're both friends and lovers."

"Me too," she whispers, a lovely tremble in her voice.

I drop down to one knee, take the velvet box from my pocket, and flip it open. "Arden, will you be my wife?"

She pauses for a moment, like she's taking it all in, but then her answer comes.

"Yes!" Her eyes shine with happy tears that spill as she clasps her mouth and nods fiercely. "Yes, yes, yes. I would love to be your wife."

My heart fills with happiness as the woman I started to fall for long ago jumps up from her chair and gives me her hand. I slide the diamond onto her finger, and she gasps, more tears rolling down her cheeks.

Her voice cracks. "It's beautiful. I love it. I love you so much."

I stand and wrap my arms around her, kissing her softly as the ladies clap and cheer. I move my mouth to her ear, whispering, "I'm so grateful I found you throwing cheese and crackers down a trail. I'm so glad I was there that day, and I intend to be there for you every single day for the rest of our lives."

Cheek to cheek, she whispers back, "It's the same for me, and I have so many plans for us."

I laugh and kiss her once more. "I do love it when you devise your lists and strategies."

She pulls back and meets my eyes. "You're my best-laid plan."

ANOTHER EPILOGUE

Arden

I've always been a planner. I like to research and plot. To be as prepped as I possibly can.

But in the last year or so, I've learned that planning is both everything and it's everything you sometimes need to toss out the window.

I was so fixated on my preserve-the-friendship strategy with Gabe I nearly missed a chance at the biggest gift in my life — love with a man who fulfills me, heart and soul.

I had to break out of my good-girl shell to snag that love.

Sometimes, I'm still a good girl. I make my husband dinner, and I love to bake him goodies to take to the firehouse and share with the other guys. Though, truth be told, sometimes he taunts the guys with them and keeps all the treats to himself, even when Shaw tries to grab them, even when Derek, when he's there, does as well. *Boys will be boys.*

I love, too, to greet Gabe when he comes home after a long shift.

But I've learned that the element of surprise works wonders on my man.

Some days I wear an apron. Now and then, I don a silky little robe. Other nights, I slip into a new bra and panty set he hasn't seen.

Every so often, I answer the door in nothing.

And each time, without fail, he picks me up, carries me over his shoulder, and takes me somewhere—the bedroom, the kitchen, the couch, the wall right next to the door one time when he was particularly pent up—and shows me how he feels about my greetings.

I suppose I feel naughty then.

Incredibly naughty.

But I've learned that naughty can be oh so very nice.

Especially when you're wildly in love with the man you can share all your dirty fantasies with.

All you have to do is ask for what you want . . . and it's quite nice indeed when you get it.

And with Gabe, I get it good.

THE END

Dying to know what happens with Perri and the guy she pulled over? Temperatures heat up for Derek and Perri in their red-hot, roomies-to-lovers romance THE FEEL GOOD FACTOR! You won't want to miss the sarcastic cop and the inked bad boy in their sexy romance!

Sign up for my newsletter to make sure you don't miss this hot new book!

ALSO BY LAUREN BLAKELY

FULL PACKAGE, the #1 New York Times Bestselling romantic comedy!

BIG ROCK, the hit New York Times Bestselling standalone romantic comedy!

MISTER O, also a New York Times Bestselling standalone romantic comedy!

WELL HUNG, a New York Times Bestselling standalone romantic comedy!

JOY RIDE, a USA Today Bestselling standalone romantic comedy!

HARD WOOD, a USA Today Bestselling standalone romantic comedy!

THE SEXY ONE, a New York Times Bestselling bestselling standalone romance!

THE HOT ONE, a USA Today Bestselling bestselling standalone romance!

THE KNOCKED UP PLAN, a multi-week USA Today

and Amazon Charts Bestselling bestselling standalone romance!

MOST VALUABLE PLAYBOY, a sexy multi-week USA Today Bestselling sports romance! And its companion sports romance, MOST LIKELY TO SCORE!

THE V CARD, a USA Today Bestselling sinfully sexy romantic comedy!

WANDERLUST, a USA Today Bestselling contemporary romance!

COME AS YOU ARE, a Wall Street Journal and multi-week USA Today Bestselling contemporary romance!

PART-TIME LOVER, a multi-week USA Today Bestselling contemporary romance!

UNBREAK MY HEART, an emotional second chance contemporary romance!

The Heartbreakers! The USA Today and WSJ Bestselling rock star series of standalone!

Unzipped, when the dating coach meets her match!

Birthday Suit! A USA Today Bestselling forbidden romance!

The New York Times and USA Today Bestselling

Seductive Nights series including *Night After Night*, *After This Night*, and *One More Night*

And the two standalone romance novels in the Joy Delivered Duet, *Nights With Him* and Forbidden Nights, both New York Times and USA Today Bestsellers!

Sweet Sinful Nights, Sinful Desire, Sinful Longing and Sinful Love, the complete New York Times Bestselling high-heat romantic suspense series that spins off from Seductive Nights!

Playing With Her Heart, a USA Today bestseller, and a sexy Seductive Nights spin-off standalone! (Davis and Jill's romance)

21 Stolen Kisses, the USA Today Bestselling forbidden new adult romance!

Caught Up In Us, a New York Times and USA Today Bestseller! (Kat and Bryan's romance!)

Pretending He's Mine, a Barnes & Noble and iBooks Bestseller! (Reeve & Sutton's romance)

The Break Up Album, the USA Today Bestselling standalone romance! (Matthew and Jane's romance)

My USA Today bestselling No Regrets series that includes

The Thrill of It (Meet Harley and Trey)

and its sequel

Every Second With You

My New York Times and USA Today Bestselling Fighting Fire series that includes

Burn For Me (Smith and Jamie's romance!)

Melt for Him (Megan and Becker's romance!)

and *Consumed by You* (Travis and Cara's romance!)

The Sapphire Affair series...

The Sapphire Affair

The Sapphire Heist

Out of Bounds

A New York Times Bestselling sexy sports romance

The Only One

A second chance love story!

Stud Finder

A sexy, flirty romance!

CONTACT

I love hearing from readers! You can find me on Twitter at LaurenBlakely3, Instagram at LaurenBlakelyBooks, Facebook at LaurenBlakelyBooks, or online at LaurenBlakely.com. You can also email me at laurenblakelybooks@gmail.com

Made in the USA
Middletown, DE
19 February 2019